Prohuman Inc.

JILL THRUSSELL

ISBN: 0993389988
ISBN-13: 978-0993389986

CONTENTS

PROHUMAN HQ

Martine was excited as she woke up and prepared for her day, today was perhaps going to be the beginning of an amazing adventure, which promised to be full of intrigue and delight. The beginning of an enchantment. She'd booked her consultation at Prohuman Inc.; she was now ready to attend her induction and to proceed with the tantalizing leisure activities she'd seen advertised on the glossy website and brochure that had arrived in the mail earlier that month.

The fact that it was the weekend, was even more fitting for her, that meant she could relax and prune herself immaculately and be adequately prepared to meet anyone interesting the opportunity may present. The brochure she'd been sent had adequately illustrated the captivating physicality of the male founder and she was making that little bit of extra effort to ensure he noticed her physicality too.

Tall with dark, rugged hair and a slim, athletic build he was in Martine's mind the perfect male. His existence enticed and encouraged her to make more of an effort. She grabbed some long, diamond, dangly, sparkling earrings from the jewelry box on the nearby dressing table and quickly put them on. They were the kind she usually only wore to attend parties, special occasions and evening events but with a possible meeting with the founder of Prohuman looming on the horizon, she felt this had the potential to be an exceptional situation which definitely required additional effort on her part.

Flicking through the brochure as she sipped on her coffee a few minutes later, she read his name once more and smiled. It sounded so masculine, scandalous and snappy. She let the words roll of her tongue as she spoke breaching the quietness of the lounge surrounding her.

"Ray Raskal." She announced boldly. "Ray Raskal." She repeated his name again, only this time in a slightly softer, more seductive tone. "It's a pleasure to meet you." She continued to rehearse her imaginary meeting with him as she glanced in the mirror on the wall nearby and raised her eyebrows suggestively as she spoke.

She nodded a few minutes later deciding that yes that would be exactly how she 'd greet him, if the chance presented itself. Flirting wasn't totally her forte as she was well aware but on this occasion she'd decided if she got the chance to, she'd definitely give a it a try. It was worth the risk to make an attempt despite the possibility of rejection, Ray Raskal was worth it.

Arriving outside the Prohuman Inc. building, she smiled as she glanced up at the splendor towering before her. The white shiny stone exterior glistened as the rays of sun bounced and reflected off the building and it seemed to spread out as far as the eye could see.

The grounds surrounding the building were immaculate, the walkways lined with well pruned trees and hedges. She knew at that precise moment from all she was observing externally, she was about to enter inside perfection. She gazed back at the parking area for a second, her car sat quietly a slight distance away from where the other vehicles were parked; alone and waiting for her return. She reassured herself as she smoothed her fitted, black knee length dress down firmly against her legs and prepared to enter the building; she was ready, she was ready to meet Ray Raskal.

Assertively she stepped forward and placed her hand on the huge glass doors, pushing them open and entering inside. A female suddenly appeared from one side of the foyer and approached her with her hand outstretched. Martine smiled and reciprocated as she glanced for a second behind her at the black marble reception desk nearby. The interior of the building was already living up to her expectations and she was fully satisfied that this was indeed a highly professional, corporate environment.

"Martine Cummings?" She asked.

Martine nodded vigorously and enthusiastically in response, impressed that the receptionist had actually known her name. The first member of staff she had met on arrival, had already struck a great first impression. Her conduct to Martine illustrated and enhanced the attentiveness, professionalism and competence she expected to be encapsulated in every pore of the Prohuman experience. Martine had been won over already, not only was the interior of the building impressive, the interior of the staff was too.

"If you'd like to follow me." She continued as she turned towards a glass doorway nearby and started to walk towards it.

Martine followed her a few steps behind obediently as they walked through the doors and down the hallway behind it. Her nerves started to kick in slightly and her hands drew beads of sweat as she walked. She was suddenly a little anxious. She began to question herself would this be the experience she thought it might be, was there anything to worry about? They walked in silence for a few more moments as the questions continued to flood through Martine's mind, casting slight shadows of doubt on her initial positivity. A few moments later however she was distracted from her negative thoughts as they arrived at a conference room towards the end of the hallway.

Martine observed as she entered the doorway it was a huge room with space and seating for at least one hundred people. Luckily however there were only four or five people seated inside and the rest of the chairs lay empty as they stood in their regimented rows, saluting each other. The chairs black, shiny exterior was almost like a uniform, as they contrasted against the stark white walls of the conference room. Relief set in as the receptionist showed her to a chair nearby and she sat down.

Everyone sitting in the conference room turned around and looked at her as she entered and she suddenly felt slightly self-conscious. She fidgeted as if trying to distract them or herself as she smiled at the receptionist thankfully, who then departed leaving Martine in the midst of the handful of strangers. Around fifteen more people were chaperoned inside over the course of the next five to ten minutes as Martine sat waiting expectantly for the induction activities to begin. She looked at her phone for a moment to check the time, unusually for her on this occasion she'd arrived early, the prospect of meeting Ray Raskal had provided her with additional motivation, pushing her to arrive on time for an appointment for a change.

The time approached for the induction to start as the conference room filled up, around twenty other people who were now seated inside it. The people surrounding Martine mainly occupied the first few rows of chairs and the rows towards the back of the large room she observed lay empty and redundant. The founder entered the room a few minutes later and Martine was delighted by his appearance and arrival, not only was he hosting the induction, he was also considerably more handsome in reality and his presence was electrifying. Ray Raskal approached the front of the room and smiled at everyone his pearly white teeth glistening like snow as the spectrums of light inside the room bounced of them. Her body started to tingle with excitement as she looked at him with intense fascination.

"If I can have everyone's attention please." He remarked as he clapped his hands together to alert the room to his presence.

A few people sitting around the room by now had started to engage in chit chat and small talk whilst they were waiting. They hadn't actually noticed Ray Raskal's entrance, therefore the clapping of his hands was a necessary but polite interruption to their conversations.

The room fell silent almost immediately and Martine's mouth began to salivate as she began to admire and absorb Ray Raskal's stature and build. He was muscular but not large and bulky, toned by not overly taut. Here he was in real life, Ray Raskal the founder of Prohuman Inc. Martine's passion for him escalated as it stirred and burned inside her as she yearned for Ray Raskal to soothe and cool her down with his touch.

Everyone in the room around her turned to face him almost immediately, giving him their full attention. Not only did his presence look amazing

Martine thought, it also commanded instant respect. Her mind started to play with her thoughts back and forth once more as she watched him for a moment, why was she here, what desire, craving and yearning was she attempting to fulfill? She pondered further as she sat watching Ray Raskal captivated by his presence, was it the experience Prohuman was offering or was it the possibility of a private liaison and interaction with Ray Raskal? Possibly she finally decided it was a little of both.

Martine shook her head at her self-analysis, she was being too hard on herself she decided after a few minutes of introspective examination. She was after all only a human being which meant she was subject to lust, desires and physical attractions. She finally accepted that she was just here to have some fun and that, that was a sufficient enough justification for indulging in Prohuman Inc. and its services. Focusing her mind back to the task at hand, her induction, she once more focused on Ray Raskal as he started to address the audience and speak.

A female coordinator suddenly entered the room, she was in her early fifties and she positioned herself next to Ray Raskal as he spoke. She was at least fifteen years older than Ray

Raskal, a moderately attractive woman with mousy brown hair which had flecks of blonde running through it. Her figure was relatively curvy and voluptuous, her nails well-manicured and immaculate. She smiled at everyone as Martine focused her gaze on her for a second curiously, she began contemplating what it would be like to work for Prohuman Inc and see Ray Raskal every day. She continued pondering how it would feel to be in close physical proximity to him and even alone together with him on occasions. She speculated further that perhaps seeing him every day might create a kind of numbness to his rugged good looks and her appreciation and enjoyment of them. Gazing at him for a second, she wondered for a moment how exactly old he was, he couldn't be a day over thirty five Martine concluded. The female coordinator interrupted her thoughts and brought her crashing back to earth by speaking through a small microphone attached to her blouse and interrupting her indulgence in the meanderings of Ray Raskal's physicality's.

"If everyone can pay attention to the screen at the front of the room please." She announced. "The main presentation is about to begin."

Her voice vibrated through the airwaves, flowing all around Martine and washing over her as it alerted and reminded her, there were around twenty other people in the conference room beside herself right now. Her initial excitement at Ray Raskal's arrival and his presence had totally distracted her and she'd almost forgotten they were even there. Their presence evaporating into obscurity as she'd become more and more distracted.

Martine questioned herself internally as she considered the possibility that the female coordinator may have noticed Martine's lack of attention as she wondered if it had it been obvious that her concentration had deviated and lapsed. Martine felt the female coordinator's gaze suddenly burn into her shoulders like a hot rod piercing her skin as if her last remark had been directly aimed at her. She felt a pang of guilt for a second as she regarded her attraction and obvious distraction due to the presence of Ray Raskal and shook her head.

Martine instantly sat up very straight in her chair as if making an attempt to convince the coordinator that she was being attentive and that her mind was fully engaged and ready to absorb the information she was about to present to them.

The coordinator looked at Martine for a moment longer with a blank expression which provided no clues to Martine on her thoughts. Martine's question remained unanswered as it dissolved, evaporated and disappeared into the realms of irrelevance. Whether Martine had been obvious or not about her attraction to Ray Raskal no longer seemed to matter anymore to the coordinator as she turned once more to face the large glass screen on the wall behind her and started to touch it.

The screen started to fill with bright images and Martine was immediately intrigued, she was yearning for something different to occupy and fill the dull hours of her nonexistent social life. Her job was boring, she had absolutely no love life and this was something new, unique and captivating. The lights dimmed around them as Ray Raskal touched a control pad in his hand to adjust them; due to the lack of windows in the room it suddenly became quite dark.

Everyone was silent as Martine gazed at the people around her for a moment. The number of participants seemed quite equally spread in terms of gender and age; varying from a young man in his mid twenties to a woman in her late sixties. Martine was quite impressed by the diversity of the other participants.

A lady in her late sixties who was seated nearby smiled at Martine as she gazed at her for a moment, her face shone and was slightly weathered decorated by a few fine lines which only slightly illustrated the many years she'd so obviously lived. The woman in question who was the sudden object of Martine's interest wore makeup that was immaculately done and she was dressed in a long flowing dress which had beige and brown tones and patterns decorating it. Her hair was an auburn brown and dusted with some reddish strands; it reminded Martine of the leaves in the autumn that tried to cling on to the trees as the winds would howl around them and try to strip them away.

Her presence encouraged Martine as she reassured herself, if she at her age could participate in Prohuman, then Martine had absolutely nothing to be afraid off. Secretly inside subconsciously Martine hoped to herself that she looked that good when she reached that age and time in her own life.

Martine continued to analyze the room around her and the other participants as she turned her attention to some of the other people around her, another male seated a few rows away caught her attention slightly for a moment. She shifted her gaze and looked at him a little more attentively for a few minutes, he was around five years older than she was perhaps Martine decided somewhere possibly in his mid-thirties. His face was relatively cute but she knew there was a huge expanse and lacking as she compared his appearance with the intense handsomeness, raw masculinity and sexual appeal of Ray Raskal.

In her mind she compared the attraction she felt for both men for a split second as she found herself staring at him, he suddenly looked directly at her as if he felt her gaze upon him. Martine felt a little self conscious for a moment as she realized she'd been caught staring at him. He smiled at her as if trying to ease her mind that everything was perfectly fine as she reciprocated in response with a tense smile that attempted to disguise her discomfort. Behind the smile, inside she was almost burning with embarrassment and humiliation however as she contemplated how he might interpret her stare. Martine began to question her own actions further for a moment as she pondered why she'd even been staring at him in the first place.

Martine reassured herself for a second as she thought about it further for a moment, he was probably flattered by her stare rather than offended, after all she thought men usually liked to be considered visually appealing and attractive. Quite often she thought, heterosexual men enjoyed women's attention and she reassured herself for a moment he was probably not an exception to that rule. It indicated interest and appreciation. It signaled curiosity. It could even be an indication of unspoken sexual desires. Unexplored unspoken words and glances now existed between them she thought, that may possibly ignite his primal male instincts and invigorate his masculine senses. She may have invoked an emotional and physical response he may wish to pursue at a later point in time.

The presentation once more started and beams of light flooded across the room as it shifted their attention back to the purpose of the induction. Everyone was instantly distracted as they all turned to face the front with eager anticipation, the stares and smiles between strangers were quickly forgotten.

Martine's eyes had started to adjust and become accustomed to the darkness of the room now but now as she quietly watched the screen in front of her the sudden brightness of the screen changing as it filled the room with vivid, vibrant images however shocked her eyes for a few seconds as the rays of light flooded around her and embraced the darkness surrounding her.

The images though bright and almost blinding, captivated her as she forced herself to endure the adjustment as her attention became fully focused on the screen once more and the images displayed on it, the range of services and attractions Prohuman Inc. had to offer started to appear and the distraction of any attractive males around her was completely forgotten for as her mind embraced the visions before her with ecstatic enthusiasm and excitement. She gasped as her senses awoke and she became invigorated. The enticing sights were captivating as she waited with eager anticipation for the induction to finish and her first taste of the actual activities Prohuman had to offer too begin.

The female coordinator who by this time had introduced herself as Athena, continued her presentation methodically as the screen flickered and changed. The screen displayed a variety of different aspects and topics which she discussed significantly in more elaborate detail as she proceeded with the induction session. She spoke for at least an hour as she covered a variety of topics regarding the Clan system, the benefits and drawbacks of each Clan, the activities you could participate in and how the various clans interacted with each other, an hour went by as her audience listened attentively and obediently.

"Socialites, Protectors, Enablers, Attackers and Freelancers are the five Clans we currently offer." She explained. "Though in the future we may offer access to more clans, for now we're focused on these five."

The Freelancers, Athena explained was the final clan group that she introduced which wasn't really a clan at all. It was more like a collective group of individuals, who participated in a free capacity and engaged in various types of activities as and when they wanted to. The other clans she explained were more structured and their activities seemed to flow around a particular range of objectives.

Martine at that point decided she'd probably join the Socialites or the Freelancer clan groups, the other clans Athena had described, sounded a bit too much like hard work to her as she contemplated the decision she knew she'd be asked to make shortly. In her mind Prohuman Inc was a way to spend her leisure time and she decided she was definitely not spending it engaging in anything that seemed too laborious and demanding. The descriptive of the Socialites and Freelancers was far more compatible with Martine's perception of enjoyment and how she envisaged engaging in an artificial social life.

The presentation ended about ten minutes later and Ray Raskal, who had disappeared completely by this point now returned. He walked towards the front of the room once more from the other end of the large conference room as he suddenly reappeared. The lights brightened and the screen at the front went blank as Ray Raskal nodded towards Athena appreciatively. She smiled, picked up some forms and pens from a nearby table and started to hand them out to the participants seated in the conference room in front of her. Martine gazed at the form that was handed to her as she looked at the questions and tick boxes occupying it that decorated the predominantly blank white space. The questions were simple and seemed to just probe her understanding of the information she'd just been shown.

"Anyone have any questions?" Athena asked as she returned to the front of the room and smiled at everyone.

Martine waited a few moments hesitantly, then as a few people around her raised their hands, she did also. She was comforted by the fact that the other participants wanted more information on particular aspects of the experience they were about to engage in and that provided her with more confidence to present her own questions too.

Athena nodded at Martine as she smiled welcoming and prompting her to speak.

"Go ahead." She insisted.

For a moment Martine hesitated, unsure if she should proceed as she hadn't been the first person to raise her hand and it seemed a little impolite to jump in front everyone else that had raised their hands before her. She was also a little nervous about being the first person to ask any questions as it put her on the spot a little. Martine contemplated for a moment the possibility that her question may be interpreted by those around her as silly perhaps, paranoid or unnecessary. The coordinator Athena sensed her nervousness and nodded enthusiastically as if to encourage her once again.

"Is this perfectly safe?" Martine finally blurted out a little unsure and worried as she searched her face for answers whilst addressing her.

Martine wanted to be reassured but at the same time she wasn't fully sure she could trust Athena's response in totality, after all Athena did work for Prohuman Inc. which meant she therefore had a vested interest in defending the very leisure system they were offering. Martine scanned her face as she tried to analyze her expression and emotions, she searched for any signs of betrayal as she waited for Athena to respond.

"Definitely." Athena remarked as she nodded vigorously in response reassuringly.

If Athena was lying Martine concluded, she'd disguised it very well. There was no hesitation or any other sign of possible dishonesty. She started to relax as she accepted Athena's face, words and answer all of which seemed to be consistent.

The youngest male in the room who also had his hand raised was next to be attended to. Athena turned towards him and nodded as she faced him and focused her attention on his face as she prepared to address his question.

"Can we interact with anyone inside the system?" He asked. "Even if they are a member of another clan or group."

Athena nodded reassuringly as she replied. "Sure you can, anyone at all. If they are unlocked and you have access to their profile." She explained as she smiled.

A few more people asked questions and Martine listened quietly as she started to complete the form she'd been given by Athena a few minutes beforehand. Prohuman Inc. was costing her $50,000 a sum which had been required as an initial sign up fee and each month, she was also expected to pay a monthly maintenance fee. It was an expensive luxury but she didn't have any kids to support or an expensive mortgage to pay, which meant she had a decent amount of disposable income she could allocate to such expenditure. Martine had decided she deserved a treat and this was the treat, she'd felt tempted and decided to indulge in.

The form though it mainly composed of tick boxes also had an exclusion clause somewhere near the bottom that required participant's signatures. The exclusion clause was quite regular and simply exempted Prohuman Inc. from liability in case anything went wrong. Martine had previously participated in a few experience type activities and it seemed pretty standard to her in terms of the kind of forms she'd usually been asked to sign. She knew the sign up to Prohuman Inc. and participation in it's offerings implied her agreement to be involved in mind manipulating and mind altering activities therefore she could understand the company's desire to protect themselves somewhat from any potential lawsuits that could arise if client expectations were not met.

The presence of the form, its contents and in particular the exclusion clause didn't alarm her and she signed it almost immediately.

The headsets they would wear to access the system, Martine was almost sure radiated some kind of electrical waves. The headset Athena had explained throughout the induction would allow them to experience touch, smell and sound as well as fully access visual stimulations. There was also a sensor which connected and interacted with each users neural processes, allowing their brains to define, control and instruct their actions and physical movements within the Prohuman system environment known as Recreation. Therefore although she'd been reassured somewhat of the safety of the activities on offer, Martine was still very much aware that this was an experimental leisure activity which may be slightly more risky than some others.

Athena started to wander round the conference room and collect the completed forms as she instructed the group on how the rest of the day would proceed.

"We'll have a break for coffee and lunch now." She said as she collected the forms and briskly shuffled them into an orderly pile in her hands.

She seemed somewhat relieved as Ray Raskal approached her to collect the completed forms she'd retrieved as she handed them to him. Everyone seated in the room started to stand now as she motioned towards them to follow her out of the room.   Ray Raskal stood in a stationary position at the front of the room as she did so which made it very obvious to everyone inside the room, he wouldn't be accompanying them for the coffee and lunch break. They filed out of the room one by one and as they passed him, he seemed to be oblivious to their exit, distracted and occupied by his own thoughts.   The group exited and entered into the nearby hallway a few steps behind Athena.   She quickly led them down the hallway as she walked briskly in front of them and back through the reception area once more. Martine observed as she walked through the reception once more there were actually six glass doors in total that all lead off to different hallways which led off in different directions. Athena strode across the reception and opened one of the glass doors at the other side of the foyer as she led them in the opposite direction away from the conference room they'd just departed from.

Whilst they walked Martine took the opportunity to ask her another question. "Will we actually be trying out our clans today?" She enquired curiously.

"Not today, we're scheduled to do the actual participation initiation session tomorrow." Athena replied as she continued to lead them down the hallway beyond the glass door they'd entered.

Martine nodded in understanding as they soon arrived at the other end of the hallway and entered inside some black shiny doors which led into a large canteen room. Similar to furniture situated elsewhere the building, the seats and tables were black and had a glossy, shiny appearance that glistened as the dim lights of the canteen reflected off them. The tables lined the walls and had long bench like seats that could sit a few people on either side. It wasn't a huge space and there were only about twenty tables inside the canteen itself; the bench like seats and tables were nestled in little alcoves and a long shiny black counter lined one wall, it had a long hatch above it which opened out from a kitchen situated at the rear. Several staff manned the counter and as they approached them, the staff smiled enthusiastically to greet them. The food was elegantly laid out in silver warming trays and a pile of plates sat at one end of the long, oblong counter. Athena encouraged them to start picking up plates and to help themselves.

The mature woman Martine had found herself gazing at earlier in the conference room in admiration and the man who'd caught her staring at him, gravitated towards her as she made her way towards the trays of piping hot food.

"What a wonderful spread. I'm Penny." The mature woman said as she extended a hand towards Martine and introduced herself properly.

Martine smiled in response and replied as she drew closer. "Nice to meet you I'm Martine."

"Ladies, I'm Jonas." Jonas interrupted as he stepped forward, he neared the trays laden with food by which they were standing as he smiled at them.

They both smiled back at him in response as he offered to serve them, he picked up a large silver serving spoon nearby and started to fill up a plate with the contents of one of the dishes, the chicken marinated in sauces, fruits and spices glistened as he spooned it onto his plate. Penny stretched her plate out appreciatively towards him and nodded as he began to fill it also. Martine approached another tray nearby and started to fill her plate with barbequed skewered prawns. She walked down towards the other trays on the counter and picked out some salad, some barbeque ribs and some fries. The food smelt delicious and Martine's mouth began to water as she quickly found a table nearby and sat down. Penny and Jonas drifted over to join her once their plates were adequately filled.

Jonas began to eagerly shovel forkfuls of food into his mouth as they made small talk and relaxed. The ambience and mood was mellow as Martine began to contemplate what the next day might bring.

"Are you scared Martine?" Jonas teased as they ate.

Martine smiled as she thought about the question she'd asked Athena earlier, she wondered if he'd remembered it.

"A little I guess." She replied as she gazed at his face for a moment inside she wondered if he was perhaps a little scared also.

His face gave no signs of fear or any other kind of emotion as he reassured her convincingly.

"I'm sure it'll be fine. After all we're not the only people who've ever done this, they've been operating as a company for a while. I checked." He insisted with certainty.

SYSTEM ARCHITECTURE

The lunch and coffee break was soon over and the induction group led by Athena, returned to the conference room once more. Ray Raskal didn't make another appearance that day as the afternoon ushered in and became their companion, dismissing the morning as it expired. Athena sat at the front of the room as she continued discussing all the different clan groups and she started noting down each individual's preferences.

"We'll reconvene tomorrow at ten am." She explained as she rounded off the afternoon session later that day.

Everyone prepared to leave as she rounded off the session and the induction attendants started to filter out of the room in groups of two or three.

Penny and Jonas hung back waiting for Martine as she fiddled around packing items into her handbag and gathering her belongings. She stood up, picked up the jacket she'd thrown over the back of the chair she had been seated on, then plucked her bag up off the ground from beneath the chair where it was situated.

"Ready?" Jonas asked as he looked at her and smiled as he wondered why women always seemed to take longer to organize themselves than men.

Martine nodded and as they made their way towards the door, she noticed they were indeed the last people to leave the conference room and that the room was now empty. All the human bodies that had occupied it only a few minutes ago had disappeared and she'd been totally oblivious to their departure. Martine sighed, that was one thing she may never change about herself, she was usually the last to arrive and the last to leave any event she attended. It wasn't intentional, she always planned to be a bit more organized and timely but somehow, something always went wrong. She'd get ready in plenty of time with all the best intentions, then she'd become distracted along the way somehow and try to fit in another last minute task, thinking that she had time to do so. The last minute task would usually take longer than anticipated and she'd wind up later than she'd planned to be. Martine usually had a bag full of various accessories that she carried with her absolutely everywhere she went; everything she needed could always be found inside that bag. Whenever she arrived somewhere and each time she left, she'd always cream her hands and check her lips which she would usually rub quickly with moisturizing lip balm before she exited.

These small quirky habits were just something Martine had always done and no matter how she was teased about it at school and college, it was unlikely these little habits would ever change.

Penny, Jonas and Martine finally vacated the room leaving Athena alone. Whilst they walked down the hallway, Jonas cracked some jokes which made Penny and Martine smile as they listened to his weak attempts at humor. Jonas to Martine seemed to be quite a simple, laid back kind of person, his sense of humor however though bearable was not outrageously funny or even mildly entertaining. She indulged politely however by smiling and nodding at his jokes at regular intervals.

The group walked towards their cars parked outside. Penny smiled as they arrived at her car which was the nearest. It stood out with its bright adornment and unusual shape, the light turquoise blue, bubble shaped car seemed out of place amongst the rows of sedan like vehicles, the pink, bubble shaped decorative patterns painted onto the exterior made it even more noticeable and different. Martine looked at it admiringly, it was quirky and unique very much like Penny was. Martine would never have the guts to drive around in a vehicle that was so different she thought as she smiled. Penny noticed her smile and nodded as she walked towards the driver's door and pressed the keyring in her hand to unlock it. The security system made a small beep as the car doors unlocked.

"This car was a gift from my daughter." She remarked. "I've had it for a few years."

Martine smiled again and nodded reassuringly, as if to let Penny know her car was fine and that its presence required no justifications or excuses.

Penny bade them farewell a few seconds later and as they watched her drive away, Jonas and Martine stood silently for a moment as if unsure what they should do next. Martine began to quiz herself silently about whether she should walk towards her car or wait for Jonas to walk her she wasn't totally sure. She froze for a second, as she contemplated what would be the most polite thing to do at that precise moment in time.

Jonas answered her silent question a few seconds later as he looked around the parking lot and then pointed towards the remaining surrounding cars he gazed back at her as he smiled.

"Which one's yours?" He asked politely.

Martine smiled and pointed towards her simple silver, saloon. It wasn't huge and very luxurious but it was suitable for her needs and handy for shopping trips. Usually her shopping was home delivered but on some occasions she still enjoyed taking a trip to nearby stores and picking up some items in person. On some occasions Martine would even make an afternoon of it and go shopping with one of her female friends. Quite often such trips would usually end with a night out afterwards. These night outs usually consisted of a visit to a restaurant for a meal and would be rounded off by a visit to a bar for a drink and a dance afterwards.

Martine knew however that more recently most of the female friends in her circle of friends were starting to develop serious relationships with significant others. The implications of their pairings meant that shopping trips and evening hangouts were becoming less and less frequent. Being that she'd treasured such occasions and that she was the only one amongst her female friends group that was still single; Martine felt the absence of those occasions more strongly and yearned for them more often than anyone else in the group did. Martine missed them and she yearned for the days when such activities were frequent and regular.

Martine pointed towards her car and they started to saunter over towards it. Jonas talked as they walked.

"That was a very intelligent question you asked." Jonas remarked. "It was good to put them on the spot that way. I'm sure many people were quite anxious and wanted to ask the same question."

"Thanks." Martine replied as she blushed a little, impressed that he'd actually remembered the question she'd posed.

"Are you definitely coming back tomorrow? Or are still unsure?" He continued.

Martine gazed at him for a moment before she replied as she began to notice that at close range he was actually a little more handsome than she'd originally thought.

"Yes I am." She replied as she nodded with certainty and smiled. "What about you?"

Martine's doubts about Prohuman Inc. had been fully satisfied now and had totally subsided. She'd been reassured and comforted by the presence of the other participants within her induction group, who'd attended the induction alongside her. She'd been satisfied by the professionalism of the staff and the environment. All these factors had appeased her mind and she eagerly began to look forward to the next induction session the next day.

Martine felt complimented by Jonas's curiosity and his determination to ensure they'd meet again. He'd definitely made an effort that Ray Raskal hadn't regarding his attentiveness towards her and she'd now noticed it and started to appreciate his efforts.

"Which clan are you joining?" Martine asked him curiously as they approached her car and she prepared to unlock it. "Have you decided yet?"

"I'm definitely more interested in becoming a Attacker." He explained. "If I become bored, they did say apparently after one month you can change clans, so if that happens I might become a traitor and move to the other side and become a

Protector." He remarked as he smiled. "Both clans hold an appeal for me."

They'd explained the one month rule to Martine and Jonas at one point during the induction. Apparently according to Athena allocating clients to clans required different mappings and users had to be slotted in to interact with different programs according to their clan groups. Athena had explained this took quite a bit of work and programming time, therefore they required an initial and ongoing commitment of one month at a time to any particular clan group. Prohuman wanted them to be sure she'd explained that they'd explored all the functionalities of their chosen clan before accepting or rejecting it after the first month's trial period. Every month after that she'd explained, they could review their choices and had the option to move around or to continue participating in their existing clan.

Martine had been relieved by their diplomacy and their accommodation of client's desires. She had absolutely no desire to be stuck in a clan she hated for too long and the ability to move around to different clans if you really wanted to at given intervals really appealed to her.

Jonas and Martine now lingered silently like awkward school children meeting in a playground as they stood by her open car door. Neither of them was in a rush to leave as Martine realized quite possibly Jonas had no other plans that day either.

"Do you fancy going for a pizza?" He finally ventured to ask as he broke the silence that had accumulated between them.

"Sure." Martine replied.

Martine had absolutely no plans for the weekend ahead at all, she'd kept it totally free due to her induction at Prohuman which meant she had nothing to do either and she gratefully accepted his invitation. It gave her some kind of comfort to know she was befriending someone that she could discuss her involvement in the Prohuman Inc. leisure activities with.

Martine's female friends weren't even aware she was doing this and she was unsure about sharing information regarding her attendance at this unusual place with them. They might think it was weird she'd decided as she retained her silence on the subject whenever they conversed in the run up to her induction. With regards to her family it wasn't even a debatable topic, there was no way in hell Martine was going to tell her parents about the latest leisure activity she was indulging in. Where her friends might think it was weird and laugh about it her parents were more likely to possibly panic and be highly skeptical about it. Martine was already skeptical enough, therefore a choir of skepticism was the last thing she'd needed in the run up to her attendance at her induction. Martine also knew the initial signup fee that Prohuman Inc. had required was already spent and it was nonrefundable, another factor which had crowned her secrecy regarding her participation in Prohuman's services.

Jonas was a providing a welcome break to the isolation she felt and Martine started to appreciate it. She embraced his efforts to reach out to her and nurture their companionship as she engaged more attentively and reciprocated.

They agreed to meet at a pizza place in town and he made his way back to his car as she entered inside hers. Martine started to drive towards the nearby exit and Jonas followed her out. Whilst driving she turned on the radio to listen to some jazz music; a sultry, rich female voice wafted through the air as she tapped on the steering wheel, entertaining thoughts about Jonas as she drove. Martine's car was actually self-driving but very often she opted to drive to her destination manually as she enjoyed the feeling off having control over the vehicle. Somehow having control of her car as she drove, reassured her and appeased her nerves. On occasions when she felt particularly lazy however she would indulge in the self-drive option however those instances were very rare.

The pizza place wasn't far away and they arrived shortly afterwards. Once they'd parked their cars in the dusty, gritty parking lot nearby, Jonas and Martine walked towards the restaurant door and entered inside. Jonas was very much the gentleman and opened the door politely and then waited for Martine to enter inside first. The pizzeria they decided upon was one of Martine's favorite restaurants in the city, the interior was adorned in a rich assortment of deep red, gold and cream tones and had golden pillars lining the rows between the tables, it reminded Martine somewhat of a middle eastern palace. The décor was visually pleasing and it calmed her as they entered inside and waited to be seated. A waiter rushed to assist them a few minutes later and showed them to a nearby alcove which housed a table and bench like cushioned chairs.

"What do you think of Prohuman so far?" Jonas asked as they sat down. "I mean in terms of the experience itself?"

"I think it's a very interesting concept, an amazing opportunity and it could be a lot of fun." Martine replied as the waiter handed her a menu and she smiled at him, she started to read it and then paused for a moment. Martine looked into Jonas's eyes, her face yielding an expression of deep sincerity and seriousness. "You can probably tell though, I do have a few reservations about the technology itself after all sometimes the impact of various technological advancements can be severely detrimental to human beings." She remarked, she paused for a moment before she continued as she realized how pessimistic she sounded as she attempted to lighten the conversation a little. "I'm trying to put my worries aside for now though as I possibly worry a little too much."

"Yeah hopefully we'll live to discuss what we did there in the future." Jonas teased playfully as the waiter returned.

Jonas quickly ordered a bottle of wine then they proceeded to select some pizza toppings; they'd decided to share a large pizza and were selecting and decorating each side with their choice of toppings. The waiter who'd been serving them disappeared once they'd finished choosing as he rushed off to satisfy their order; whilst they waited, they continued to talk.

"Do you think we're weird for wanting to do this?" Jonas asked a little nervously.

Martine smiled a little surprised at his frankness, he'd asked a deeper question she'd not dared to even think about, never mind discuss with anyone. A question she'd not even dared to verbalize or ask herself. She gazed at his face for a moment before deciding he was definitely a little more complex and interesting than she'd originally suspected.

"Not really, weirdness is a subjective concept, don't you think?" She finally replied. Inside Martine realized her response was an attempt to reassure herself, whilst reassuring him.

The pizza arrived soon after and as the waiter placed the food he was carrying down on the table Martine's mouth began to water as she gazed at it. The oil glistened on the top as the smell of tomato and fresh herbs, wafted through the air and filled their nostrils tempting them and quenching the edges of their hunger. Jonas thanked the waiter who departed a few seconds later as he disappeared to another part of the restaurant. They started to serve themselves eagerly and hungrily and Jonas made small talk as they ate.

"What do you do for a living?" Jonas enquired.

"I'm an interior designer." Martine replied. "What about you?"

"I'm a software engineer." He replied. "That's why I find Prohuman particularly interesting, it explores systems that are new to me, in ways I've never experienced before."

Martine nodded in understanding as she listened and he continued to discuss his work a little further.

The late afternoon danced into evening like wild seeds scattering in the wind as Jonas ordered another bottle of wine and they discussed various aspects of life. Two hours later, they left the restaurant as Jonas settled the bill. The sharp, brisk breeze of the evening air hit Martine in the face as they exited; her skin had become warm from the wine they'd consumed but as soon as she stepped outside, the cold air provided a sharp shock to her body. She shuddered as the winds cold, chilly grip embraced the naked parts of her flesh and dove into her pores like an unrelenting predator ravages its prey.

Jonas and Martine made their way quickly back to their cars nearby which were now parked side by side in the parking lot. They paused outside their respective car doors for a moment to unlock them as Jonas continued to make jokes about the wine they'd consumed. Martine smiled politely as she considered Jonas a little further, he seemed an intelligent, reflective man but some of his jokes verged on awful but she knew that was something she could probably never tell him. When it came to feelings, Martine knew that politeness was sometimes the better option than blurting out blatant blunt comments that were unnecessary and hurtful.

They parted a few minutes later as Martine stepped inside her car and agreed to meet the next morning. She smiled as she began to drive home, glad that she'd made the effort to attend Prohuman Inc. after all. She'd started a new adventure, she'd met someone of the opposite sex who was slightly interesting and made a new female friend all in one day.

Although she still had a few fleeting thoughts of a possible romance with Ray Raskal, Jonas had now actually started to grow on her in terms of the effort he made and how comfortable it was to be around him and he'd began to titillate her interest as the prospect of a romantic interlude with him danced in the shadows of her mind teasingly. Jonas possessed a likeability that she was starting to feel drawn too; almost like wearing a pair of comfortable slippers at home he made her feel completely at ease. Ray Raskal on the other hand was very exciting in an exhilarating manner which captivated her but also made her a little nervous. She'd observed when he was in close proximity and he moved closer to her, that her hands would break out in a slight sweat and her body would tremble gently. She loved the thrill of Ray Raskal but felt more at ease in her companionship with Jonas.

There was a stark difference between the two and the different reactions Martine's body had to each one. Could she forgo the electric appeal of Ray Raskal for the safe, reliable Jonas? Would she become more attracted to him with time? Those questions occupied and danced in her mind as she drove home in through the quietness of the evening.

At this point in time she was completely unsure who would end up having the biggest influence over her romantic choices and which one she would ultimately desire to enter into a romantic relationship with. They were both attractive, just in very different ways, she decided.

When she arrived home, she parked the car in the driveway and made her way into her house. The questions she was asking herself were not questions that had to be answered today, she thought as she touched the fingerprint pad that secured her front door. A few seconds later a green light shone at the bottom of the fingerprint lock pad and the door clicked as it unlocked to indicate she could enter inside. Martine stepped inside and embraced the warmth that emanated from inside the doorway as it welcomed her home and wrapped itself around her like a blanket.

The next morning arrived soon enough as the sunrise shone in through the windows brightly almost as if it sought to remind her of her appointment and awaken her like an impatient child waiting for a treat. Martine made her way once more back to Prohuman Inc. headquarters. When she arrived, she parked her car in exactly the same space in the parking lot as she had on the previous day. Once she exited her vehicle she noticed that Penny and Jonas's cars were already there and that there were a significant numbers of cars in the parking lot indicating that she was possibly verging on being late. The glass exterior doors stood awaiting her touch as she opened them and entered inside briskly and glanced at her phone for a moment to check the time, she smiled, she was indeed running a few minutes late as usual. Martine shook her head and hoped that she hadn't missed anything important.

The receptionist smiled at Martine as she entered inside and motioned towards the nearby glass door Martine had entered inside the previous day that led to the conference room.

"They've already started. Go straight in." She remarked.

Martine nodded appreciatively and rushed towards the door quickly as she understood that this time she would have to find her own way to the conference room alone.

"Thank you." Martine replied quietly as she turned back for a second just before she opened the glass door that faced her. She was still a little worried about her lateness.

A few minutes later as she entered inside the conference room however, she was instantly reassured that her lateness was not a problem as Athena smiled at her to welcome her. She pointed towards a nearby empty chair and nodded, as she urged Martine to occupy it. Martine cast her eyes quickly over towards the chair nearby as she noticed that there was a headset situated on top of it. She nodded and walked over towards it as she participated fully with Athena's request without further hesitation.

Martine started to envisage and imagine what it would be like for a second to delve into the different areas and experiences, the engineers at Prohuman Inc. had created as she sat down. Her hands started to sweat slightly as she held the headset excitedly; this was the moment of realization, the beginning of her journey into the unknown. The start of her meanderings into the depths and abyss of an imaginary existence and a world that did not actually physically exist.

Ray Raskal to Martine was a pioneer, there was no doubt at all about this in her mind. Her perception of him was that he was unparalleled in comparison to other men she knew, he was a visionary, a prophet and an explorer, taking human beings to unexplored and uncharted lands that humanity had never visited before. Martine could sense Athena reveled in this environment as she worked alongside Ray Raskal. It was an unusual vocation, intriguing and unique. For a second Martine felt slightly inferior as she considered her own work, which was definitely far less glamorous and exciting.

Martine gazed around the room for a few minutes and Jonas nodded his head towards her, to acknowledge her entrance. Martine nodded in response and smiled in appreciation. Penny caught her eye and Martine smiled at her as she noticed her seated in a chair situated a few rows away. Penny smiled as she held the headset in her hands and raised it slightly in excitement as if raising a glass to toast someone in celebration Martine almost started to laugh as excitement began to well up inside her but as she glanced back at Athena's serious face once more, she restrained herself.

Athena tapped the microphone, then started to relay instructions to everyone as they focused their attention on her and began to listen, they hung onto her every word as she spoke. They became her captive audience as they listened appreciatively, they all knew that compared to anyone else in the room she was the only expert in this subject matter and that fact commanded their full attention.

"Has everyone made their final decisions on the clans you'd like to join now?" She enquired as she finished instructing them on how to wear the headsets. "A few of you yesterday were still a little unsure and needed a bit more time to decide." She remarked.

Athena looked towards Jonas, Martine and a few other people situated in the conference room as some of them nodded in response. Jonas had decided to join the Attackers. Martine and Penny had decided to join the Socialites. Martine even though she didn't feel attracted to the Attackers Clan could fully understand the appeal that particular clan group would hold for most men and even for some women. The Attackers provided people who wanted it with a primal masculine outlet, allowing males and females clan members to express and realize aggressive, destructive desires that so often lay hidden and suppressed within their interiors and their inner realms of consciousness. Desires that could not be realized or fulfilled in reality.

Athena picked up a headset from the podium at the front of the room and started to illustrate to everyone how the headsets should be used. The room fell silent once more as everyone focused intently with total concentration on Athena as she spoke.

"This is how you actually wear the headset." She explained as she put it one on, she then pressed a switch on the side. "This switch activates the sensory interaction between you and Recreation, the Prohuman Network." She continued. "To experience the full enjoyment of Recreation, this must be switched on at all times." She verified.

The induction participants in the room all nodded as they listened and watched Athena totally captivated their eyes followed her every movement as she spoke almost in a hypnotic trance like state.   A few seconds later Athena stopped explaining and started to walk around the room, she assisted people as she helped them put on their headsets.   Jonas smiled at Martine as Athena strode briskly over towards her.   Martine quickly started putting the headset on before she arrived in order to illustrate her attentiveness to Athena's instructions.

"I'll see you soon." Jonas remarked.

Martine smiled and nodded gently due to the fact that the headset was now actually situated on her head; the thought of nodding too aggressively worried her as she had no desire to damage the headset or knock it out of place.

Athena continued to speak as she approached each person and attended to them, she gave more individual guidance to each client as she made her way around all the participants in the room.

"The entrance sequence will load automatically once the headset is on and the switch activated." She explained. "Each time you leave and re-enter Recreation you will enter into the same point you last exited from."

The headsets were unlike anything Martine had ever seen before. They were almost spiderlike in shape with many dark black protruding legs that were almost like thorns, that wrapped themselves around their faces leaving just a small gap at the front. A small visor dropped down to fill the gap and nestled inside it once they were situated on a participants head and fully covered their eyes. Once she touched the switch on the side as per Athena's instructions, she immediately found herself standing in a large white hallway type room. The walls and floor surged as silvery white strands ran through them in a constant gush, like waves of water that flowed as they yielded the whims of the currents within an ocean.

Five doorways were situated directly in front of her as she noticed some of the other induction clients arriving around her at regular intervals. Finally all the participants from the conference room were present and Athena also appeared. The doorways were strange in the sense that they just composed of a silver outline. Everyone around her looked slightly strange and different as Martine observed them curiously and glanced at their faces and bodies. Their skin now appeared to be either a shimmering bronze, a matte chalky white or a shiny, glossy black. Everyone's skin was now clear and perfect with no lines, blemishes or scars. Their clothing had also now changed and they were all either dressed in black, bronze or white garments made of leather strip pieces, stitched together. All the men now were now absolutely bald, whereas the woman had hair that was now either black, bronze or white as the strands glimmered and shone.

Martine smiled at Jonas and Penny who she could still easily recognize despite the changes in their physical appearance. Penny's skin was now bronze and she looked much more youthful without any off the fine lines Martine had previously observed and Jonas's face was now a chalky white, his face actually seemed to look a little more handsome as Martine gazed at it curiously for a moment. Martine glanced down at her own legs and arms and noticed that her body also was now a chalky white and that strands of her hair were now a shimmering bronze. The leather clothing she wore was bronze in color and she smiled as she examined herself and everyone around her a little more closely. Inside Recreation she was relieved to discover, everyone looked cosmetically more attractive than they did in real life. Their artificial existence would provide them with a reassuringly more pleasant cosmetic form which some people she was sure would appreciate.

Martine had been slightly worried at some point prior to the induction about the possibility that they wouldn't look good inside the system or that entering inside it would induce some strange kind of lighting that magnified every imperfection on their faces and bodies. However those fears now vanished as she embraced her new look enthusiastically.

Athena smiled as she watched the group nearby acclimatize to their surroundings and change in appearance. A few seconds later, once she was satisfied everyone was ready she made her way towards a nearby door. She turned to face them and started to instruct everyone on the next steps they would take.

"Attackers, you will go through this door." Athena instructed. "You simply walk into the doorway." She explained as she motioned towards the silver outline nearby. "The door doesn't open."

Jonas smiled at Martine and she nodded encouragingly as he took a few steps forward. Martine watched him and a few others disappear into the Attackers doorway nearby and deliberated on when she would be shown the Socialites doorway. She continued to listen to Athena as she waited patiently to discover which door she'd have to enter to become part of and participate for the first time in the clan group she'd chosen.

"Enablers, go through that door." Athena continued as more people smiled, nodded and responded. "Protectors you go through this door." She explained as she pointed to another doorway. "Freelancers you go through this door." She remarked as she took a few steps towards one of the two final remaining doors.

Everyone disappeared through their respective clan doors until just a handful of people remained in the hallway. Athena then turned to face them and smiled.

"I guess you must all be Socialites." She concluded. "The final door over there is yours."

Martine's stomach turned a little with nerves and excitement as she made her way towards the door Athena had pointed towards. Her evenings were often long and lonely and she was slightly relieved that she had found a welcome distraction to indulge in that would occupy and brighten those dull nights, an activity to lavish and fill the empty corridors of the redundant hours she often spent alone and bored at home. Recreation she felt would provide a fresh, invigorating hobby that would be fun and engaging. She could access this world every evening if she so desired from the comfort of her own home or anywhere else she chose to go; the flexibility and ease of access to Recreation appealed to her immensely as she prepared to enter the doorway Athena had pointed her towards.

Briefly Martine gazed back at Athena's face before entering the door for a moment, slightly nervous for a second about actually stepping through it. Athena smiled and nodded at her to encourage her as if she sensed her nervousness. Martine smiled as her mind was reassured. She turned back to face the door once more, took the final step and walked through it as the doorway consumed her and Athena disappeared from sight.

The step over the threshold brought Martine abruptly into a round, narrow spiraling passageway. Unlike the hallway she'd just come from the walls in the passageway glistened predominantly with black, glossy, bright, shiny strands, a few brightly colored strands also ran through the black walls at seemingly random intervals. She took a step forward and suddenly found herself moving forward without actually walking any further. The ground beneath her feet moved almost as if she was standing on a conveyor belt. Martine found herself being transported at a gentle speed as the silent mechanism moved her through the black tunnel like passageway that surrounded her. It carried her around the many twists and turns which led to an unknown destination.

A few minutes later Martine found the floor was no longer moving and that she was now surrounded by a large white expanse. She stepped out onto the white floor that preceded her as she noticed Penny who was standing nearby speaking to another women that had also been within their induction group. The women in question that Penny was speaking too, Martine had only briefly noticed at the induction sessions and they hadn't actually spoken yet. She had mousy, dull brown hair, wore quite old fashioned, frumpy, odd looking clothing and she didn't seem like the kind of person that Martine usually acquainted herself with or made any kind of effort to get to know.

Her appearance hadn't enticed Martine to make any particular effort to meet her up until that point in time and she'd had felt very little interest in her. Martine knew she was a little superficial but accepted that this indeed was one of her failings she often acknowledged it as she succumbed to it on a regular basis. Her eyes seemed dull and lifeless as Martine gazed at her curiously for a moment as she wondered if perhaps she was a time traveler who had been dropped into their time zone by accident. Perhaps she decided she came from another time. Another era. A forgotten existence.

Penny smiled as Martine walked towards them and introduced her eagerly. "This is Martine." She explained to the plain looking woman standing next to her who despite the cosmetic enhancements that the Reaction system provided, still somehow managed to look a little plain and less attractive than those surrounding her.

"Nice to meet you Martine. I'm Mavis." Mavis remarked as she addressed Martine in a warm, inviting manner as she stretched out her hand in an act of friendliness.

Mavis's politeness immediately caught Martine off-guard as she reciprocated and shook her hand. For a moment Martine felt a little ashamed of her harsh judgements, regarding Mavis's physical appearance and her obvious lack of visual appeal. Not everyone could be visually pleasing to the eye in terms of physical attractiveness and not everyone was naturally filled and brimming with the excitement and joys of life. Martine realized that she had perhaps judged her, rather superficially and rebuked herself internally. Mavis was humble, very approachable and being that they were all in a strange environment, Martine began to appreciate her efforts to be friendly. She had ultimately put Martine at ease a bit more in this strange, exciting, turbulent, dynamic environment.

One thing did puzzle Martine for a moment however as she continued to talk to Penny and Mavis. What exactly was the appeal of the Socialite Clan to Mavis she mused as the unspoken words teased her mind and prodded her curiosity gently. Most people she'd observed from the induction group who'd selected the Socialite Clan, like Penny and herself, seemed to be a bit more outgoing socially however Mavis definitely wasn't.

Martine smiled as she pushed the thought to the back of her mind a few seconds later and attempted to rationalize the situation; Recreation was actually the ideal environment for people to discover themselves and experiment socially without any fear and perhaps Mavis desired to explore some unexamined, suppressed, extroverted urges she possessed inside and the

Socialite Clan would provide her with the ideal opportunity to do so. It would enable her to be more outgoing and risk more active and extroverted social interactions, Martine concluded without actually embarrassing herself or bearing the possible effects of doing so in real life.

A man also stood nearby the group as they talked, he was in his early fifties and had also chosen the Socialites clan; he stood stationary positioned close to the group of women but did not utter a single word to them even when they turned their attention towards him and faced him. He seemed to be rooted into the ground as if he was an oak tree or a sentry on guard, outside a royal palace. His face didn't flinch, he didn't move a muscle and he didn't even glance at them once, not even for a moment out of curiosity. The blank expression and lack of interaction seemed slightly odd to Martine as she gazed at him curiously for a moment, she pondered as to whether they should disturb him and introduce themselves or not.

Penny noticed him also but unlike Martine she'd decided that she was not going to accept his lack of interest in their presence. She walked over towards him smiling gently as she drew closer as if to press him for his attention.

"Very exciting isn't it?" She asked him enthusiastically as she approached.

Martine attempted to hide her amusement at Penny's actions and daring curiosity, but betrayed herself as a smile broke out onto her face

The man looked at Penny for a moment, nodded briefly for a second and then resumed his fixed stance once more, aloof and strangely distant. Martine rolled her eyes in irritation at his lack of response to Penny's obvious effort to reach out to him. She wondered how on earth he would cope with the activities in the Socialite environment later on, being that he couldn't even embrace or accept Penny's attempt to introduce herself to him. Perhaps she decided, he'd be an anti-social, Socialite.

Martine soon bored of pondering over his lack of interest in them as she decided to explore the white expanse surrounding them. She walked about fifty steps in front of her, away from the entrance they'd arrived from, where to her surprise she found a fountain with white bench like sofa's around the circumference.

"Penny, Mavis come over here quickly." Martine called as she urged them to come closer excitedly, glad to have found something to break the monotony and whiteness of the space in which they were standing.

Perhaps she thought for a moment, this was what it was like to be stranded in the desert surrounded by miles of miles of sand, looking for an oasis, only in this instance the desert composed of this curious white expanse which seemed to be infinite.

Martine before finding the fountain had almost thought for a moment that the whiteness around them stretched into eternity. She had observed no other signs of life or any other kind of construction in front of them that she could see. Speculating for a moment, she'd even began to contemplate that perhaps Prohuman was attempting to trick them and that perhaps maybe there was really nothing beyond the doors they'd walked through. The fountain she'd stumbled upon this fountain which had only appeared visible when she was five steps away from it had appeased her mind as she embraced its presence. She wondered for a moment if it was actually a mirage and if her mind was perhaps tricking her somehow. It had appeared as if from nowhere and Penny and Mavis were totally oblivious to its existence and smiled as they approached and discovered it also.

Martine drew closer to ascertain if its existence was indeed real. Penny and Mavis who had rushed over by now excitedly, joined her eager to explore the discovery she'd made. They gasped as they found the fountain and smiled. Penny rushed forward and sat down quickly on one of the sofa type benches situated around the fountain with no apprehension or hesitations at all. She beckoned towards Martine and Mavis to join her as she sat. They joined her and turned to face the fountain as they sat and watched the sparkling, silver water drops fall down in front of them for a few minutes in awe and silence. It seemed somehow magical and enchanting.

Martine leant over towards the base of the fountain and ran her fingers through the shallow pool of water as she attempted to evaluate its existence and reassure herself that the fountain was indeed real. She smiled. Her fingers felt wet and tingled as the lukewarm warm water teased them as she dipped her hands in and out of it.

Martine smiled again at her own thoughts as she reminded herself of where she was and what she was actually doing. The fountain was only as real as it could be in the environment they were currently existing in she contemplated. Deep within her, she realized as she reminded herself nothing actually inside Recreation was truly real in the physical sense. Recreation and everything in it inhabited an artificial plane of existence which would only exist as long as it was allowed to survive by those who controlled and participated within it.

THE CLANS

Martine, Penny and Mavis sat quietly by the fountain as they admired it for a few minutes longer, a few seconds later a female coordinator appeared in front of them almost as if from nowhere as if she'd been formed from the vast white expanse surrounding them. She walked towards them out of the whiteness as they looked at each other surprised as she approached.

"Good you're all here." She remarked as her mouth opened and revealed a huge, flashy, sparkling grin.

Her comment reassured them that she'd indeed been expecting them and reassured them instantly. Martine couldn't help but notice her teeth were immaculate as they shone, along with her matching hair and nails which were all golden and shimmered as she walked. Her outfit was an electric red, it shone, glittered and sparkled as she drew closer.

"I'm Socialana." She explained. "I'm here to show you around."

"Are you here all the time?" Martine asked curiously as she wondered if perhaps she was another coordinator like Athena.

"Yes I'm here all the time. Recreation is my home. I'm a program." She explained in response. "I was created to interact with participants of the Recreation system inside the system itself. Outside Recreation I don't actually exist." She clarified.

Penny, Mavis and Martine seemed slightly amused as they smiled and nodded and listened to her speak, her voice lilted almost like a bird in song and was extremely high pitched. Penny pointed back towards the direction they'd come from where the solitary man had been standing and smiled at Socialana.

"What about him?" She asked curiously.

Socialana smiled.

"Don't worry I'll come back for him." She explained. "For now let's just focus on you three. I'm here to show you around, interact with you regarding your needs and provide suggestions in case you are bored or stuck and need some additional stimulation." She explained.

Martine felt relieved as she listened, relieved that there was indeed some kind of assistance available within this strange new environment. Whilst she was excited about exploring it and all the possible interesting things it appeared to offer, the fact that there was some kind of guide and support in case of any urgent issues, appeased her and calmed her.

The mission statement on the Prohuman Inc. brochure had stated:

Our mission is to add value to human life by fulfilling our clients unsatisfied needs through leisure and recreational technologies, designed to entertain and enhance their social interactions.

Martine had been extremely impressed by the Prohuman Inc. mission statement and had signed up almost instantly upon reading it. Meeting and interacting with the program Socialana and the fact she was a program, somehow made perfect sense to Martine as she considered further for a moment the environment they had been provided access too.

The Recreation system Martine imagined and speculated had to be manned twenty four hours a day as that was the duration that it was accessible to clients. Being that this was a high tech solution it made sense that Prohuman would manage the internal system through some kind of simulated program and high tech staffing solution. It was very cost effective she thought, it meant Prohuman could save the efforts of the paid human staff and reduce their involvement in the performance of repetitive internal system tasks, it was a clever way of maintaining the system. It reassured her as it was another indication of the high standards of perfection and professionalism Prohuman Inc. seemed to offer and adhere to.

Athena had advised the attendees on the first day of their induction, that if they really couldn't make a decision and choose a clan, there was a program called 'Allocation' that could assist them. The program devised activities for clients and then evaluated the most suitable clan group for them based on their interactions and performance. No one in Martine's induction group however had required that kind of assistance and they'd all managed to arrive at their clan selection decisions quite easily which meant therefore that the 'Allocate' program had not been utilized throughout their own induction sessions.

The Socialites Clan had instantly appealed to Martine as the ideal choice for her personally as they built things; networks, connections and friendships, the activities offered seemed to her far more enjoyable, appealing and preferable than the more destructive and aggressive nature of the tasks undertaken by the Attackers. Attackers it had been explained were predominantly involved in conquering type activities and the Protectors would oppose them as they took actions to defend those they were protecting against those attacks.

The Protectors mainly performed tracking, chasing and defense action tasks. They often had to camouflage themselves, creep through tunnels and perform stealth missions.

Attackers attacked both Enablers and Protectors, who were their main target groups. The Socialites and Freelancers were neutral and were not a target, though Freelancers also at times had the option to join in and participate in Attacker, Enablers and Protector's missions. Socialites on the other hand only had the option to join in some Enabler missions.

Enablers performed maintenance tasks for all the other clan groups. They maintained the theme park; they picked up litter, made sure the rides worked, painted the area and equipment, manned the rides and various stalls inside it and performed other general maintenance tasks throughout other parts of the system. Their range of activities also included their own puzzle tasks which were focused on enabling development. Other areas they could explore Athena had explained at the induction, involved creative and encouragement tasks and missions, where Enablers could actually get involved in creating and recommending tasks for other clans members to participate in and provide words of encouragement to individuals they provided enabling support to.

Martine, Penny and Jonas had discussed which clans appealed to them in detail when they'd attended their lunch on the first induction day. Penny and Martine had both agreed that after the Socialite Clan, the Enablers Clan appealed to them slightly more than any of the other clan groups. They'd agreed that if either of them ever actually left the Socialites Clan, the Enablers Clan would be their most likely destination and second choice.

Athena meanwhile was back in her office. She'd finished with the client group for the next couple of hours and she'd left them in the capable hands of the programs that manned the Recreation system and various clan groups. The internal Prohuman system itself was simply called Recreation and the guides had been programmed to show any new inductees around as soon as they arrived.

Ray Raskal had named the system Recreation as he'd felt it expressed the main mission of Prohuman. Yes the system utilized futuristic technology, experimented with neural processes and inner human chemistry but essentially at its core it was a recreational provision. He'd decided that was the most suitable name for the internal framework he'd created and it had been called Recreation ever since the formation of Prohuman Inc..

Athena smiled excitedly as she received a message from Ray Raskal on her pager. He was requesting her attendance at the nearby staff canteen. She prepared to meet him as she pulled a mirror quickly out of her bag nearby and checked her hair, face and lips. Once satisfied that her appearance was satisfactory to engage in his presence she rushed out of her office and headed towards the canteen to meet him.

A few minutes later she strode into the canteen confidently as she smiled at Ray Raskal who was seated at the far end of the room. She was somewhat surprised by his request as she knew the canteen was a not a place that Ray Raskal frequented often. He usually preferred to call down to the canteen and one of the serving staff would actually deliver food directly to his private office, where he'd consume his meals in privacy. Today however, very unusually he'd broken that rule and Athena was curiously wondering why.

Ray Raskal invited Athena to sit down with him at the table he occupied. Athena did so graciously as one of the serving staff Grecia; a large, beaming, red cheeked woman in her late fifties rushed over to attend to them immediately as she noticed Athena's arrival. Grecia offered to serve Athena lunch but she declined. Athena knew that she'd be bringing her induction group to the canteen for lunch in a couple of hours' time before they left that day and she had no desire to fill her stomach with a huge meal or anything too substantial at that moment in time. She would eat with the induction group she was supervising and wanted to avoid anything too heavy. Athena however was enjoying the individual attention she was receiving from Ray Raskal and had no desire for that to end to abruptly. In order to retain his presence, prolong it and secure his attention for as long as possible, she quickly decided to order a late breakfast instead.

"Can I have a pot of coffee and some pancakes Grecia please." She said after a few minutes of quiet consideration.

Grecia nodded, scribbled the order down on a pad in her hand, then rushed away to prepare her order.

"How are the new group of clients settling in Athena?" Ray Raskal asked her as they found themselves alone.

"They're doing very well." Athena replied. "They're inside Recreation at the moment with the program guides."

Although she explained to him where the client group were, Athena knew deep within there really was no need to elaborate much further. Ray Raskal had obviously known that she wasn't with the group of inductees as he'd called her to meet him. Athena was also very much aware that Ray Raskal had access to every part of Recreation, he could see everything that happened within it and he had full access to all the security systems that guarded it, which meant he could see the precise location of any person within Prohuman headquarters or in the surrounding grounds at any given moment in time. Her explanation of the inductees whereabouts, she realized was quite unnecessary as she began to feel a little awkward and self-conscious for a moment.

Grecia arrived back at the table a few seconds later with a tray, situated on it was Athena's pot of coffee and the pancakes she'd requested which eased the awkwardness of the moment. Grecia placed the plate of pancakes and two pots of coffee down on the table gently, one of which she'd brought for Ray Raskal, Athena smiled graciously as she did so. Ray Raskal nodded appreciatively at Grecia and she departed leaving them alone once more.

Ray Raskal glanced at Athena and smiled for a moment. She wondered internally for a few seconds as they drank the coffee, if she was perhaps too old for him as she gazed at his physique admiringly. Athena and Ray Raskal had absolutely never gone down the road of physical exploration before and she wasn't sure they ever would. Athena knew, he was her employer and that exploring such attractions or the possibilities of such a romance was risky, unless he made the first move.

"I'd like you to visit the Recreation engineering control room and see how the new clients are settling in." Ray Raskal instructed as he looked at Athena sharply for a moment, the smile fragmented almost as if it was being shattered like a smashed glass whose pieces dropped to the floor revealing a frown in its place, his remark indicated to Athena immediately that this indeed was not a suggestion but a command.

Ray Raskal's request was unusual and not one he usually made but he'd decided recently that this action was indeed necessary and should form part of the induction process. The staff he felt needed to be a little more thorough about inductions now as client subscriptions were growing and needed to be monitored more intensely. Ray Raskal wanted to ensure that new clients were settling in properly as soon as they participated in the Recreation system and that they were happy with Recreation from the first moment they interacted within it.

Athena smiled in agreement and nodded. She appreciated Ray Raskal's thoroughness and dedication to his work. He was unlike most other men she knew who were very often distracted and preoccupied by women, clothes, fast cars and illustrations of wealth and power. He held his power and wealth silently, not exhibiting it or displaying it to the world at large or even much to those around him.

A few minutes later Ray Raskal gulped down the remainder of his coffee and stood up as he prepared to leave. Athena took that as her cue and stood up also, she knew that Ray Raskal would now disappear and it was unlikely she'd would see him again for the rest of the day. Their moment of interaction for today was over and she wouldn't have the chance to indulge in any pleasantries with him again until another day.

Ray Raskal nodded as and then left the room. Athena sighed as he disappeared from sight a few minutes later and sat back down as she carried on drinking her coffee alone. She finished the coffee as she appreciated the pancakes she'd just consumed, they'd been a welcome break before lunch and filled the gap in her stomach that had formed since she'd been running slightly late that morning and missed breakfast. She stood up and smoothed down her dress as she prepared to face the engineering control room to tackle her next task.

Athena's dress was the standard female uniform that Prohuman Inc. provided. The felt material was black and the dress had thick white stripes that ran down either side. The female uniforms were quite simple but elegant and looked extremely professional. Athena had been relieved when she started working at Prohuman Inc. that the uniforms were relatively pretty and not ugly eyesores. She was extremely self-conscious and often worried about her physical appearance. The men had similar uniforms provided to them, a simple black shirt with white stripes down the front and plain black trousers. Ray Raskal himself usually wore a dark suit, coupled with a white shirt and rarely diverted from this.

Athena arrived at the Recreation engineers control room a few minutes later and entered inside. She was technically the highest ranking employee in the hierarchy at Prohuman Inc. aside from Ray Raskal himself, being that she was a Chief of Staff. Each department had its own departmental manager, however she was technically the manager of all the managers as well as a department manager off her own team. The implications her position meant that she could access most areas of the building without any prearranged appointment or meetings being requested and that she had the right to question anyone she found there.

The engineer control room was being manned by two staff as she arrived. Reuben a male in his early thirties and Enoch a more mature man in his late forties, sat inside the room as she entered inside. They were oblivious to her arrival as they were seated facing a large screen on the wall at one side of the room. Reuben's build was slight and his appearance attractively adorned with coal black hair, jet black eye lashes and pale olive toned skin. He looked as if his roots stemmed from a country in Asia, though Athena knew he'd been born in the USA. She'd never actually bothered to ask him to find out which country he came from as she rarely engaged in personal conversations with any of the staff she managed. Athena preferred a more regimented, management style, which meant she maintained her distance and never indulged in what she deemed as inappropriate interactions with those she regarded as her subordinates.

Enoch's skin was dark brown and she was aware that he originated from an island situated somewhere in the Caribbean though precisely which one she'd never ventured to ask due to the barrier she retained. When he spoke his accent however did occasionally made her smile as the deep, bass, lilt of his voice sounded almost musical and soulful. Enoch and Reuben discussed their after work plans amongst themselves as she approached them quietly.

"I'm going out for a rum and some cocktails with a woman I've admired for a while." Enoch explained to Reuben.

Enoch was the proverbial bachelor of the Prohuman staff team and all his work colleagues knew this well and his lack of desire or plans to change his status. From what people could see Enoch enjoyed his freedom and he enjoyed it immensely. Reuben on the other hand was much more settled and had actually been married to the same woman since his college days.

"I'll be taking the wife out for dinner tonight." Reuben explained.

They suddenly noticed Athena's presence as she stood between them and sat up quickly and abruptly, surprised that they hadn't noticed her entrance. Reuben and Enoch both knew that Athena was not one to take lightly and when she entered the room you paid attention to her immediately. She was reasonable and polite most of the time but if you encountered her on a bad day or took her politeness for granted, she could lash out and quite often staff would very quickly find themselves on a disciplinary unexpectedly. She was known for being quite strict and her temper could flare if she felt someone was taking advantage of the company or of her. Athena was very protective of Ray Raskal's empire and all the Prohuman staff she managed knew it.

"Do you need any assistance?" Reuben asked politely as Athena strode over to the screen on the wall nearby and started to survey it.

"I need to see how the new inductees are doing within Recreation." Athena clarified. "Just a quick scan nothing too complex. I just have to make sure they've arrived in their respective clans and are settling in well."

Reuben and Enoch nodded as they started to touch some dots on a smaller screen nearby built into another wall as they focused on a list of names that loaded onto the screen in front of them. Athena watched them as they accessed images of Jonas, Martine, Penny, Mavis and the other clients she'd conducted inductions for that weekend. A few minutes later she nodded at Reuben and Enoch to indicate that she was satisfied. Athena had been reassured that the group were finding their way around the system and that the internal programs were serving their purpose and doing their job, Ray Raskal's instructions to her had been fulfilled sufficiently she determined. A few seconds later she rushed back out of the control room in a sweeping fashion as she vacated it and left Enoch and Reuben alone once more.

Reuben and Enoch looked at each other anxiously for a few seconds as they shut down the various windows on the screen and made their way back to the seats they usually occupied. A few seconds later they both sighed with relief as they glanced at each other and smiled.

"I almost thought for a moment we were in trouble." Reuben said quietly. "I mean Athena hardly ever comes down here."

Enoch nodded. "I know and when she does there's usually an axe to grind with someone." He replied in agreement though his voice wavered slightly tinged with tension and nervousness he'd worked at Prohuman for a while and had become comfortable with his role, job and work routine and had no desire to disturb it.

"Do you think she'll come back?" Reuben asked as if he was a little worried also. "Do you think there's something more serious going on?"

"Nah." Enoch replied as he shook his head and smiled as he attempted to reassure them both. "Usually if there's a problem, she would say it straight out. She's not the type of woman to hide her anger."

"You almost sound like you like that." Reuben teased him playfully.

Enoch stood up, smiled and stretched his body, then began to pace around the room.

"You never know one day Athena could be blessed and her body lavished with personal adoration from the Enoch love engine." He remarked playfully as he teased. "I still got some mileage left in this old motor and I could definitely take her for a decent test drive." He paused before continuing. "All night long."

Reuben laughed as Enoch drew nearer.

"I like the fiery ones, they always scream louder when you hit them with the love stick." Enoch said quietly as he leant down and whispered in Reuben's ear.

"She'll have you on a disciplinary if she hears you saying that." Reuben warned him playfully as he smiled.

Enoch sat back down in his chair once more and leant back. "Nah, it's not that serious man. She'd probably laugh secretly at the attention. Every woman likes to be admired. It's natural human nature." He explained.

Reuben was glad for a second that he was married, dating was complicated and he appreciated that he no longer had to do it. He'd met his wife at a college and they'd been together ever since. Olivia his wife was simple, pretty and quite quiet. They'd planned to start having children quite soon and he was looking forward to being a father. The thought of pursuing the joys of fatherhood with Olivia filled him with excitement and eager anticipation. He couldn't wait to consummate their marriage with their own offspring and he knew she was looking forward to becoming a mother also.

"We'd better do some maintenance on the programs." Enoch said as he touched the large screen nearby and several images of males and females filled it.

Reuben nodded in agreement as the images filled the screen in front of them and he focused on it intensely. When it came to work and maintenance both Reuben and Enoch knew it required their undivided attention. Prohuman though a relatively pleasant place to work was the empire of Ray Raskal and from the minute they'd joined the company he'd made it absolutely clear to them he expected total perfection from them in the delivery and performance of their tasks.

Unlike the human participants within Recreation, the bodies that appeared on the screen in front of them were electronic program stimulations, which meant their appearance was slightly different. Enoch smiled as he observed them standing in a line on the screen in front of him. Socialana, Shield, Destroyer, Builder, Lancelot, Interact, Allocate and Moderate all faced him silently and still almost frozen like statues and blocks of ice awaiting his commands, instructions and interactions. Enoch had loaded all the main system programs responsible for most of the maintenance work inside Recreation keeping them highly tuned and fully functioning was an essential part of the Engineer's roles and something Enoch and Reuben took very seriously.

The programs bright clothing and skin coupled with perfect frames were immediately recognizable and stood out as they glowed with an slight aura surrounding each of them. Their skin tones varied some were silver, some gold and some were transparent but their bodies glittered in a range of colors almost like diamonds and other precious stones. Reuben smiled as Enoch gazed appreciatively at Moderate, Interact and Socialana and drew closer to the screen.

"Trust you to focus on the female programs first." Reuben teased.

"I'm a hot blooded male and they're hot. I helped create them remember, I made them that way. I made them hot to give me something to enjoy whilst I worked." Enoch replied playfully. "They're my bits on the side. No matter what woman I finally settle down with, they'll always be my bits on the side." He explained as he nodded enthusiastically. "Anyway you should always look after a lady's needs before a man's when you're a gentleman, it denotes manhood."

"Their programs." Reuben teased.

"They're very good looking programs. They're always here and if you ever had the chance to have a session with them, it would probably be extremely wild and hot." Enoch explained.

Reuben shook his head as he laughed, they started to access the maintenance menus and a repair utility program appeared a few seconds later on screen in front of them. The repair utility program differed vastly in appearance and was a far cry from the glittery, sparkling attractiveness of the interactive client programs. Repair, as he was titled, was a short stumpy male. His hair was dark and rugged and he was always dressed in a pair of dull, red brick, dungarees with a dark shirt underneath them, his appearance was simple and plain, a far cry from the extravagancies that adorned the other programs surrounding him. He carried a large red toolbox with him that was almost half his size in height, whenever he appeared or was summoned by engineers. Repair smiled politely to greet them as soon as he appeared on the screen.

"Good day Repair." Enoch remarked as he observed him walk to the middle of the screen and stand in front of the other programs.

"Greetings Enoch. Which repairs would you like me to start with today?" Repair asked.

"Let's start with Socialana." Enoch replied. "She's my favorite, she should come first."

Reuben shook his head and began to laugh at Enoch's response as he sat down on a chair nearby and watched as Enoch started to engage fully with Repair and they began to perform the daily maintenance tasks.

MARTINE'S SELECTION

Martine prepared with eager anticipation to access Recreation for the first time from the comfort of her own home alone, the first step into the unfamiliar, exciting, enticing world beckoned her as she gazed at the headset on the chair beside her. She stood up, strode across the room and dimmed the lounge lights and the early evening darkness dulled the room as she thought about the implications of participating in Recreation without the comforting presence of Penny and Mavis beside her it was exciting but a little nerve racking. Martine decided once inside Recreation she might try to find them inside the Socialite Clan area so she would not be totally alone.

Jonas was working late and was on call, therefore meeting him inside was not going to be possible on this occasion. Though he'd been added to her visible contacts list she knew she wouldn't actually be able to meet him inside Recreation if he was not actually present at the same time she was. Perhaps she thought if Mavis or Penny were available and present when she arrived in Recreation she'd invite them to complete a social challenge with her. She picked up the headset and looked at it for a moment as she took a deep, sharp breath and prepared herself to enter Recreation.

Once she'd placing the headset on her head, she paused for a moment and turned as she noticed the Prohuman Inc. brochure sitting idly on the table in the center of the room. She glanced at it for a moment, enticed to pick it up as the image of Ray Raskal stood out on the glossy front page. Martine sighed as she wondered if she would actually ever become closer to him and more intimate with him. Perhaps she concluded Ray Raskal and her attraction to him was an urge and desire that would remain unfulfilled into eternity. Martine reflected back to the induction day where they'd actually met in person for the first time, that first sexual tense, intriguing moment, she remembered he'd actually smiled at her for a second and she cherished his attention towards her. Aside from that brief interaction however she realized there were no actual real indications that Ray Raskal had actually noticed her in a way that signaled or illustrated that he was even remotely interested in her in a romantic capacity. The reality was he hadn't actually done anything that exceeded or went beyond that which was probably usual towards a customer off his business and deep down within her though she yearned for a more significant truth she knew the reality.

Jonas on the other hand had been more forthcoming, she'd noticed he was making a real effort for her and she'd decided to indulge him; she wanted to give him a little more time before she indulged or attempted to make a serious effort to push the boat out and test the waters properly with Ray Raskal.

Once the headset was firmly on her head Martine pressed the switch on the side and the visor slid out from the spider like strands of the headset and covered her eyes as she prepared to enter into Recreation. Martine's surroundings began to disappear as the simple but elegant home she resided in started to evaporate around her.

She prided herself on her home, the decoration was relatively unique being that she was an interior designer, she'd facilitated her skills to make her home look as spectacular as she could on a pretty minimal budget. The two tone black and white corner sofa took up a large space in the lounge and one of the walls was home to an electronic mural with a beach and palm trees that swayed as the aqua blue waves lapped up gently onto the shore it provided the room with a calming and relaxing ambience. The color scheme was white, black and gold and the sandy beach blended in well with the decor of the room. Situated on one side of the room, in a corner was an small alcove which housed her comfortable chair, whose wooden arms were painted gold, the interior of the chair was filled out with comfortable golden padded cushions.

The sofa was situated in the lounge for the comfort of any guests whereas the comfortable chair was there solely for Martine's occupation. She spent most of her time in the lounge, curled up on it, nestled in her alcove. Usually she was armed with a glass of wine and a meal as she watched the large screen entertainment system nearby.

Guests that visited her home absolutely never ever asked to sit on the comfortable chair in the alcove, it was as if they automatically understood it was special and reserved only for Martine's presence. Sometimes she even wondered if some people actually even noticed it was there at all, being that it was tucked away in a remote corner of the room it was barely visible from the lounge entrance.

The table in the center of the room had a black glass top and the base it rested on consisted of a sculpted statue made out of white marble. The statute itself appeared to be a male cherub but it was slightly unclear whether it really was as it also bore a slight resemblance to a few other mythological creatures and Martine was never really sure exactly what it was.

Other rooms in the house were decorated and furnished in much brighter colors, but Martine enjoyed the fact that the lounge was mellow and peaceful, it helped her to relax and unwind more easily after a long day at work. Her bedroom had a huge feature wall situated within it, painted in a deep burgundy tone, the bathroom was decorated in a deep honey gold and her kitchen a bright buttercup yellow.

She'd picked everything in her home herself and adorned her bedroom with a beautiful, classic black and white, Italian furniture bed set. The king size bed was accompanied by a luxurious, lavish, matching wardrobe and dressing table. Not many people actually had permission to venture into the privacy of her bedroom, therefore for a while now she'd been the Italian bed set's sole admirer.

Work had been hectic and demanding that day and Martine had looked forward to having an injection of some light relief and fun that evening in the form of Recreation. Jonas had promised to call her once he finished evening call duty but she knew deep down, it would be pretty late by the time that happened. Martine had resigned herself to spending the evening at home alone as she prepared to have as much fun as possible within her new imaginary playground.

The lounge inside her home by now had totally disappeared and fully evaporated around her as she found herself once more in the Socialites area in exactly the same spot she'd exited from on her last visit. She entered into the nearby lounge a huge white room with sofas strewn around it, there was a large fountain in the middle of the room and the walls were lined with capsules. Upon arrival she was relieved to find Mavis seated on a sofa inside the lounge. She smiled and greeted her with familiarity as she entered inside.

"Fancy hanging out?" Martine enquired.

Mavis looked at her and nodded eagerly as if to welcome her companionship. There appeared to be no one else in the lounge area beside the two of them and Martine had no idea how long Mavis been sitting there. Quite possibly Martine's entrance provided Mavis with a very welcome distraction from her solitude and thoughts, she concluded.

According to the induction, she'd learnt that at any given time there could be many other people in the lounge alongside her but that she may not be able to actually see them. The main reason for their invisibility was because within Recreation you were only able to unlock access to people once you'd succeeded in various challenges and only then would the people you selected become visible to you and you to them.

Martine had been permitted to select five profiles of people she could see and interact with at any time without having to complete any challenges as had the rest of her induction group. The people who had attended her induction group were also automatically added to her visibility list and aside from those twenty five people, the

Allocate program within Recreation also randomly picked five other people within her clan she could also instantly interact with. Which meant that Martine automatically had thirty people she could interact with. Tonight however it appeared as if none of the other people in Mavis's or Martine's visibility list were available, which meant they only had each other for company.

Martine and Mavis had only paid for the basic package as had Jonas and Penny which meant their visibility limits and access to the system were relatively similar. There were two other types of packages the leisure and luxury packages, these packages granted subscribers wider access to more users and a more extensive range of leisure activities. When they'd signed up for Recreation they'd all decided to opt for the basic package due to the heightened costs of the other two packages which was beyond the scope of their budgets.

"Is there anyone else here?" Mavis replied. "I mean people we can't see."

"You're guess is as good as mine. If you can't see them, it's unlikely I'd be able to see them either. I mean we're both basic subscribers?" Martine teased. "I'm here though and you can see me. I can't see anyone else."

Martine started to walk towards an alcove nearby that contained her capsule and Mavis smiled as she stood up and followed her.

"Whose capsule should we jump into? Yours' or mine?" Martine asked.

Mavis looked at her thoughtfully for a moment.

"I don't think it matters really." She replied.

"True we're getting bogged down in unnecessary bureaucratic details." Martine replied as she smiled and led her into her capsule eagerly.

Martine's capsule was the closest and the most convenient therefore it made sense to them both that they should enter inside hers. They walls of the large capsule lit up all around them as they walked in. A menu appeared in front of them as a control pad arose from the ground nearby, once it was full erect it stood to attention motionless, ready to be utilized.

"What do you fancy doing?" Martine asked. "A logical or social puzzle or a physical endurance challenge?"

"I think perhaps a logical or social puzzle, I don't fancy doing anything physical or tiring today." Mavis replied.

Martine nodded in agreement and understanding, she was also feeling the effects of fatigue on her body and wasn't quite up to facing anything physical tonight either. Even just the thought of physical activity made her feel weary, even though she was sure actually participating in something active within Recreation would probably not actually be tiring. She reminded herself for a moment that their interactions within Recreation were not actually physical real. That meant that activities they engaged in did not actually require physical labor by their actual physical bodies. Nonetheless they both decided to opt for something less physically strenuous and she smiled at their subconscious reluctance towards physical activities at that particular moment in time.

Part of Martine's inner being still yearned for the presence of Penny, who's companionship she was starting to enjoy. Martine was beginning to appreciate her more and more as they spent more and more time together and was now actually beginning to miss her when she was absent. Martine had no idea where she was however or when she'd next make a visit to her life. She pushed the thoughts of Penny to the back of her mind as she prepared to fully engage in the evening's activities with Mavis.

From the menu that appeared on the capsule wall in front of them, she selected the two preferences they'd agreed upon and then picked 'Random Selection' which meant the system would generate and select a puzzle for them. It was the lazy option but both Mavis and Martine were in a lazy mood and welcomed the automatic selection on their behalf.

A few seconds later the entrance of the capsule closed around them as the white walls in front of them began to evaporate and become a deep, scarlet red.

"What are we supposed to do in here?" Mavis asked as they gazed around the larger room curiously.

"I'm not totally sure." Martine replied with uncertainty.

They waited for a few more moments until suddenly a square object appeared in front of them, it had strange designs on it and the floor around them suddenly became colored with shaded squares like a draughts board. Some more squares began to appear much like the first one and then darker squares appeared on the floor nearby in patterned formations. The lighter squares began to depress into the ground leaving gaps and spaces between them.

"I guess we have to push the squares into the correct holes to complete the patterns." Martine concluded as she watched intrigued as the room and floor changed around them.

Mavis smiled and nodded as they started to inspect the squares and look for the corresponding patterns to complete the puzzle. They began to push blocks around and carried on doing that for a while as they inserted, rotated and changed their position until they fitted into the puzzle. Finally they completed the puzzle and the floor lit up as it seemed to swallow all the squares into it and they disappeared before their very eyes. The puzzle once completed seemed satisfied as it departed rapidly leaving them alone once more in the room. A few seconds later they found themselves once more inside Martine's capsule as words appeared in bright letters on the wall in front of them 'Challenge Complete.'

A female voice sounded out from the walls of the now empty capsule as it surrounded them, for a second they were startled by its presence, it seemed unfamiliar and foreign to them as they listened attentively. The voice didn't sound like Socialana and neither of them recognized who it actually was. Martine was unsure for a moment if the voice was actually a human voice or perhaps the voice of another computer generated program speaking to them.

"You are now entitled to your first reward as you have completed the puzzle successfully. Thank you for choosing Prohuman." The female voice stated. "My name is Interact and I'm one of the Recreation moderator programs." She explained. "I maintain and allocate the rewards to system users for successful completion of challenges and puzzles."

Mavis smiled as Martine giggled. Interact's voice sounded very soft, smooth and seductive and they'd both noticed it's enchanting tone immediately.

"I wonder what kind of rewards they'll give us." Martine asked Mavis as they huddled together.

A few minutes later a screen appeared in front of them that immediately answered her question. The screen was split into two. One side had Martine's name on it and the other Mavis's name. The list of choices underneath were exactly the same on each side of the split screen and they began to look at each choice curiously as they contemplated each item on the lists in front of them further and speculated as to which one was preferable option to them.

- A visit to the Recreation Theme Park.
- Unlock five more user profiles to interact with.
- A one on one interactive session on Social skills with a system program guide.
- A romantic liaison with another user.
- An attendance pass for the next Socialite Ball.

"Please select the reward you prefer. You're rewards are available from your maintenance menu and you can access them and utilize them at any time." Interact continued to explain.

Martine smiled as she looked at the various options surprised by the variety and nature of the offerings on display. She was intrigued by a few off them as she began to wonder what attending the ball and visiting the theme park would be like. Finally she decided to opt for unlocking five more user profiles so that she'd at least have a bit more flexibility to engage in activities with more people. Martine knew she couldn't always rely on the presence of Mavis or Penny when she was in Recreation, they simply wouldn't always be available when she was and that factored heavily into her final choice. They had their own lives as she did and their schedules were not always going to be compatible with hers, Martine thought.

Mavis had decided to select the same choice and as they picked out the option on their lists by touching the wall, the selected menu options lit up for a few seconds then vanished.

"You're rewards have been saved."   Interact confirmed.

The capsule door reappeared a few seconds later and opened as they started to make their way back out towards the Socialite lounge. They bade their farewells to each other a few minutes later as they both decided to call it a night. Martine seated in the lounge, pressed the switch to turn off her headset and removed it as she found herself alone once more and the emptiness of her lounge embraced her. She started to prepare to retire for the night. The evening she decided had been fun but now she was exhausted and she yearned to embrace the inner sanctuary of her bed.   Sleep was just a few steps away and it called out to her gently as she made her way out of the lounge, tired and satisfied that her evening had been enjoyable.

The next day Jonas called and invited her for dinner.   She indulged him and accepted his invitation willingly.   He suggested a Malaysian restaurant somewhere in the heart of the city, a suggestion which appealed to Martine's taste buds immensely. After work she rushed home to shower and change before she prepared to meet him. Her body felt riddled with hunger as she rapidly slipped on an elegant, black dress with gold, shimmering specks decorating it.

Two hours later Martine and Jonas sat in the restaurant as they waited for their curries to arrive, Martine hungrily snacked and nibbled small sticks of chicken satay as they drank glasses of wine and indulged in small talk. The restaurant itself was furnished and decorated beautifully with bamboo screens, black and cream furniture and the alcove their table was situated in, offered them a glimmer of privacy as they talked. Martine approved as she glanced around at her surroundings in an appreciative manner. It was not often she appreciated an interior as much as this one, being that she was an interior designer her approval of the restaurant's internal décor meant a lot as she made a point to compliment the restaurant staff about it as they served her.

Jonas was actually dressed quite formally for the first time since they'd met and was actually wearing a suit and tie. Martine contemplated as she admired his apparel that this was the most attractive she had ever seen him look.

"Are you seeing anyone?" Jonas asked curiously as the small talk turned towards more serious matters.

Although he wasn't asking her abruptly to be in a relationship, Martine could sense the possible romantic intentions that laced his question. Deep within she knew they'd only met recently and he didn't actually know her position regarding her circumstances, situation or relationship status, it therefore made sense he would ask if he wished to clarify that information.

"I'm very single at the moment." Martine replied as she smiled and drank some more wine.

Martine's response seemed to relieve him as she noticed he relaxed a little. Her answer to Jonas didn't actually mean however that she'd be interested in a relationship with him but at least now he knew, that the road to courtship was clear if he wished to try and pursue one. Jonas changed the topic almost immediately after the question he'd posed and started to discuss work, Prohuman and a few places abroad he'd visited as the waiter brought the main courses they'd ordered and they started to eat.

Martine smiled, he'd been brave enough to approach one of the major questions in the area of romance but he'd decided not to proceed to the next logical question. Perhaps he was unsure off her interests in him or his feelings towards her or perhaps he was worried about making a commitment to dating or perhaps he was waiting to see if their romantic interests naturally aligned with time. She really couldn't be sure. When could one ever be sure of the intentions of another she thought, even when their questions, thoughts and emotions were expressed openly. Standing bare and unguarded with no barriers, naked and exposing your inner most self to someone else was not something everyone could do easily and not something anyone ever usually did with everyone they had a romantic interest in.

The evening ended soon after and Martine smiled as they departed. The food had been good but the rest of the evening pretty uneventful as far as dates went she decided. If he did have a romantic interest in her, which by now she was pretty sure he did, it would probably take him quite a bit more effort to really clinch her interest fully she thought.

The next day Martine called Jonas to politely thank him for the outing and to make sure he felt appreciated. It had been a nice evening and she'd really started to enjoy his companionship. Deep within however Martine was glad he hadn't probed her further regarding her dating status however; she was still uncertain about the relationship potential between them and whether or not she actually wanted to commit to an actual relationship with him either now or in the future.

A couple of days later, Martine accessed Recreation again. She'd been bored and since her date with Jonas she'd done nothing much but work. Martine decided it was time to have some fun once more as she slipped on the headset and prepared for her session. She nestled back into the comfort of her comfortable chair and touched the switch on the headset to access Recreation. Immediately she found herself once more back in the Socialite lounge.

When she entered the lounge she found a message waiting for her as it flashed on a large screen on the wall in front of her impatiently demanding her attention, she touched it to access it curiously. One of the great things that Martine loved about Recreation and the Prohuman system was that you only had to think of a movement and it happened. You didn't actually have to move externally at all. The headset tracked your eye movements and the messages your brain wanted to send down your neural passageways before they were actually transmitted to your muscles and intercepted them. The Recreation system actually absorbed these messages which meant your body moved within it but your external muscles didn't actually move at all. Recreation interrupted the messages as it captured them, interpreted them and enacted them, translating them into clients movements within the system.

The message displayed more fully on the wall as she touched the flashing icon in front of her. She was asked to select five members she wanted to have access to as per the reward she'd collated on her previous visit from the challenge she'd participated in with Mavis. Martine smiled as she started to meander and flick through the profiles she could choose from. She finally picked out three male and two female profiles from the list of about thirty profiles she was shown. The female profiles she picked out were women she thought she may get along with based on the information displayed to her, whilst the male profiles on the other hand consisted of handsome, attractive looking males that she may possibly feel a romantic attraction towards.

When she'd looked through the profile list she'd been presented with she'd noticed that there were a lot more female than male profiles offered to her to select from. That made sense to Martine, she was after all in the Socialite Clan and it was only logical that her clan's membership would skew more heavily towards the female gender. She began to wonder if perhaps she might run out of male clan members to select from at a later point in time once she'd exhausted the fewer male profiles within her clan group. Martine deliberated further as she pondered as to whether she might be able at some point to access to select visible profiles from other clans and started to speculate on how they would interact if she could.

Jonas was in the Attackers Clan and she hadn't actually discovered yet how she could interact with him within Recreation. He'd been added to her visibility list as he was part of her induction group but they'd never accessed Recreation at the same time yet so she was still a little unsure of how that would actually work in reality. They'd probably work it out at some point in time somehow later she concluded. She gazed around the lounge and found Penny seated on a sofa nearby. She was relieved by her presence as the thought of hanging out with total strangers didn't quite appeal to Martine just yet. She wasn't quite comfortable enough within the Recreation system itself to do that and she wanted to become a little more familiar with it first and all its functionalities, before interacting with people she didn't even know within it.

Penny smiled as Martine approached her.

"How are you?" Penny asked as she stretched out her hand to welcome her.

"I'm great thanks and you?" Martine replied.

"Great." Penny nodded enthusiastically as Martine sat down beside her.

"Have you been trying out the system much?" Martine asked.

"Yes." Penny said as she smiled. "I even went on a date the other day. It was interesting." She explained enthusiastically.

"Really?" Martine asked intrigued by the thought of a virtual blind date. "Who did you go with? Where did you go? Was it fun?"

Penny smiled and started to provide an explanation. Penny had entered Recreation the evening Martine had been out on her real dinner date with Jonas. She'd performed a challenge alone and had completed it, Penny had then selected a romantic date as her reward. Recreation had then allowed her to pick a random male profile from one of ten profiles or given her the option of selecting a male user profile from those she already had on her visibility list. Since there were no men she knew utilizing the Recreation system aside from Jonas, who she'd felt was way too young for her, she'd picked out one of the random recommendations the system had suggested.

The man in question had been interesting and charming enough, Penny explained to Martine. He'd made pleasant conversation as they'd visited a restaurant inside Recreation and then watched a movie together in a small cinema. Afterwards they'd gone for a walk in a nearby park and spoken for a while.

"It was strange and though he seemed nice enough, I was a bit put off I guess." Penny continued.

"Why?" Martine asked curiously as she wondered what could have possibly put her off.

"He just seemed to be a little bit tense and a tad rough." Penny remarked. "I'm not sure why it was just a few things he said that gave me that impression."

Martine nodded in understanding as she thought a little more about men. Quite often they did have a more masculine side and she could understand how Penny's soft natured personality might be slightly intimated by it and any signs of aggression and roughness.

"Let's go to the theme park." Penny suggested as she smiled at Martine. "I have a reward remaining."

"Do I have to have one too?" Martine asked curiously as they stood up and prepared to go walk towards Penny's capsule situated nearby.

"No you don't. I can invite you and take you along as my guest." Penny explained. "I checked."

"Sounds amazing. Let's do that." Martine replied excitedly.

They entered inside and the door of the capsule closed behind them as a list of options appeared on the wall in front of them. Penny quickly selected 'Access Rewards' then picked out the 'Visit to Recreation Theme Park' option using the control gear stick that was now protruding from the ground nearby. Martine smiled with excitement as she realized she would actually be able to access a visit to the theme park sooner than she'd anticipated by piggybacking on Penny's reward.

The walls of the capsule now turned a deep, scarlet red and as Penny made her selection they evaporated around them and the theme park gates appeared in front of them. The gates were black, solid iron, huge and spectacular as Penny and Martine looked at each other in glee and giggled. They rushed forward as they entered inside, brimming with enthusiasm excitedly like children who'd discovered a new toy. The theme park itself was buzzing with life as they arrived. Whoever they were unable to see in other parts of Recreation was now fully visible to them here. Men and women flooded the theme park all around them, in groups, couples and some alone. Many were busy eating candy floss, toffee apples, pancakes with chocolate, burgers and hot dogs as they walked.

Penny grabbed Martine's arm excitedly as she pulled her towards a ride and they climbed up onto the platform. The small circular carriages scattered around the round bumpy floor, contained small bench like seats that were surrounded by a higher back. They climbed into one nearby and sat down as music started to play in the background and the ride began to move.

Unlike traditional rides at a theme park these rides did not have safety bars on them, which surprised Martine initially. She thought about it a bit more however and decided that safety bars were indeed in this situation totally pointless as the rides weren't real and presented no real danger to their actual, real physical bodies.

The carriages began to move round and round, faster and faster as they maneuvered up and down; they span round and round the large horizontal wheel floor as Martine clung onto Penny and giggled. They swung and slide from side to side as they laughed with glee and delight. A few minutes later the ride ended and the music stopped. Penny and Martine laughed as they climbed out of the carriage a little dizzy as they tried to retain their balance. Once their feet were back firmly on the ground, they started to make their way across the grass towards another ride excitedly.

They stopped midway at a caravan trailer like stall with an open window, where they collected some toffee apples and hot dogs that were on offer. The woman who served them smiled as they approached, her cheeks were red and glowing.

"What would you like dears?" She asked as Penny and Martine stood at the window of her caravan stall.

"Two hot dogs please and two toffee apples." Martine replied as she stood next to the open window.

Martine observed the woman attentively for a moment whilst she walked up and down inside the caravan trailer, collating the necessary items of food in order to fulfill their request. When a few minutes later the woman returned to face them she held hot dogs and toffee applies in her hands as the rich smell of the juices, wafted out of the open hatch towards them and filled their nostrils. Martine smiled excitedly as she handed the items to them. They accepted their order graciously and started to eat their hot dogs almost immediately. Martine paused for a moment after a few seconds and gazed at the woman who'd served them once more her eyes clouded slightly by wisps of curiosity.

"Are you a program?" Martine asked a little confused.

"No dear." The woman explained. "I'm Imelda, I'm an Enabler. I'm a real person."

Martine nodded in understanding. "I thought so. Thank you very much for the hot dogs and toffee applies." Martine replied appreciatively.

Penny and Martine began to walk away towards the ride they'd been heading towards.

Whilst they walked they carried on eating and talking.

"How did you know she wasn't a program?" Penny asked curiously. "I wouldn't have noticed."

Martine chuckled and shrugged as she smiled. "Not sure, woman's intuition I guess, I just felt like she was a real person. Or as real as you can be in here." Martine explained.

Penny and Martine quickly finished the hot dogs and toffee apples, then made their way to the ride nearby. Martine wanted to try as many rides as possible but she knew they really didn't have time. They both had work the next day and they both knew that was the one thing that Recreation and Prohuman could not change, the passing of time. Time did not actually stand still whilst they were there. The hours, seconds and minutes continued to tick away and the evening headed towards expiration as they enjoyed themselves regardless of their desire that it should remain still and stagnant.

Finally Penny surrendered to tiredness and called it a night. She was the first to cave in to the mental fatigue they were both beginning to feel as their interactions in the theme park started to slow down. Physical tiredness was not actually present but interaction within Recreation for significant periods of time did seem to cause mental fatigue and that affect struck Martine as she suddenly noticed how mentally drained she too was starting to feel. Martine smiled and teased her gently not wishing to leave the enjoyable evening they were engaged in that had somehow become a friend she had no wish to depart from.

"I have an early start." She explained.

"That's fine. I understand I do too. I'm just trying to push for as many seconds as I can. It's just so much fun here." Martine replied as Penny took her arm gently and led her back towards the theme park gates.

"I know. Probably too much fun." Penny groaned. "I'm getting so distracted. I'm so tempted to turn up to my appointment late."

Martine chuckled as they made their way towards the park gates once more. Their night had been fun but she knew deep within she too was ready to sleep. She decided to surrender to her own tiredness also as they walked out of the theme park gates and the capsule's bright, red walls once more surrounded them.

They entered back inside the lounge and Penny hugged her gently as they prepared to depart. Martine reciprocated warmly.

"Until next time." Penny remarked as she released her.

Martine nodded as they parted and she switched off her headset. Unlike the usual kind of parting where people usually walked away from each other, inside Recreation it was different. Inside Recreation people just disappeared once they switched their headsets off.

Penny watched Martine disappear, then a few seconds later switched off her headset as she found herself once more back in the privacy off her own lounge at home alone. Penny smiled as she thought about the evening she'd spent with Martine. She'd really had fun and was looking forward to seeing Martine again.

Penny wasn't the type to make fixed arrangements and she liked to keep her social schedule flexible, which was why she hadn't made a plan with Martine regarding their next meeting. Martine she'd assumed would also have her own real social life outside of Recreation and she felt making such appointments might end up restraining them both from any real life commitments they may need to service and attend too. That was the main reason Penny had left their next meeting intentionally, open and unplanned it meant neither of them were tied to obligations they may later regret due to other demands on their time.

Penny enjoyed Martine's company and appreciated the fact that they'd both taken time the first day they'd met to get to know each other. They'd both extended the hand of friendship out to one another and the results of that initial interaction Penny was now beginning to feel a warm embrace from as their friendship began to bare delicious, satisfying fruits that quenched her desire for human companionship.

JONAS'S JAUNT

A week had passed by since Jonas's initial induction at Prohuman where he'd met Martine. He still hadn't actually had time to utilize the Recreation or its facilities to indulge further in personal time with his headset since then. Jonas's curiosity was mounting however and though his work schedule had been hectic over the weekend, he finally found a spare moment and made some time to interact with the technology he'd been so intrigued and captivated by.

He contemplated as he touched the shiny, black spiderlike headset gently before picking it up as he pondered for a moment as to whether he should call Martine and invite her to meet him inside the system or not. He was in two minds, partially tempted to do so and partially unsure whether he should as his mind teased him with thoughts of uncertainty, brimming around his confidence and pricking it mockingly. Martine had only just met him and she might conclude he was clingy, needy and desperate, if he persisted in calling her every time he had a few spare moments of leisure time he thought.

He reached a final conclusion a few seconds later and decided to give her a bit of space. His journey and venture inside Recreation today would be on this occasion alone he decided. He put the headset on decisively and prepared for the unknown encounter he'd been eagerly anticipating as he sat down on the sofa in his lounge.

Everything around him was quiet, the simplicity and functionality of the furniture situated in his lounge, reflected his simple life. Everything inside the room was functional and the furniture around him was dark brown in color. The kitchen which adjoined to the lounge had matching dark brown furniture also and the cream walls around him complimented it sufficiently. Jonas knew his home was a typical bachelor's pad and that detail was displayed obviously in the minimalistic décor and furnishings that surrounded him. He was indeed a single man, who was quite used to his single lifestyle and his simplistic home. It wasn't large and spacious but it was satisfactory to the needs he had and that to him for now was sufficient. Sometimes he pondered about perhaps buying a larger home but in the end he'd decided to wait until he found a partner that he was finally committed to marrying. The bigger home and a marriage commitment to him were aspects of life that went together hand in hand like two lovebirds that accompanied each other wherever they went inseparable and tied with bonds of loyal devotion. At the moment however he knew this was a topic that wasn't even on his agenda; he wasn't even dating anyone, never mind in a stable enough relationship to contemplate marriage. At regular intervals he would visit his mother and she would tease and nag him gently about settling down and finding someone serious.

"You need to meet someone nice and settle down Jonas. There's more to life than work." She'd say as she scolded him playfully.

Jonas knew however romance and marriage was a little more complicated than she thought for him. He often questioned himself and his own decisions, regarding how he would know who the right person was, how he could be sure and how he should determine what it was he was actually supposed to be sure about. Those prickly questions often plagued the passageways of his mind, as they provoked dissatisfaction and uncertainty in his romantic decisions. Romance was an area that Jonas had always been a little bit confused about and the years of aging and maturity hadn't managed to break that confusion or clarify anything more for him with any certainty. He was a logical man and romance to him ultimately seemed almost illogical.

Jonas pondered for a moment as he hesitated and thought a little more about Martine, she was certainly pleasing to the eye and very attractive. From his perspective there was definitely an attraction yet deep down he knew Martine hadn't clearly indicated a mutual attraction or romantic interest in him. Up until now most of the interactions between them had been purely platonic and there were no obvious signs to Jonas that he could see for now that clarified that anything deeper existed. No green lights, no welcome signal that could push him into the area of certainty was there to reassure him that Martine actually wanted him and that he could pursue a romantic relationship with her. In his mind he was well aware that attraction and romantic interest had to exist mutually. If it was not mutually present, it was unlikely a relationship would survive the trials of endurance such a long term commitment required. It was really too early to tell he decided as he pushed thoughts of Martine and romance to the back of his mind and slipped on the headset he was still holding in his hands eagerly.

Once he switched on the headset he quickly found himself in the lounge area of the Attackers clan within the lounge where he found two people seated on one of the dark, black leather sofas scattered around it. One of the occupants was female and the other was male and as he entered the large lounge, the male stood up and walked towards him to greet him.

"Hi I'm Corbin." He said as he stretched out his hand to greet Jonas.

The gesture of friendship was appreciated as Jonas smiled and welcomed it, Corbin had disintegrated the icy, quietness that surrounded them and warmed the empty space around them like an frozen icicle melts in the rays of the sun.

"Hi I'm Jonas." Jonas replied as he smiled appreciatively.

The female who was situated on another sofa nearby at this point stood up and made her way over to them. Jonas's attention was immediately diverted as he salivated lustfully at her physical appearance. She was tall, stunning, elegant and strikingly beautiful. Her body was perfectly contoured and her approach excited him. She was lean with athletic curves and her hair was a dark, glossy, jet black. Her skin was a deep, dark bronze color which shimmered as the ray of lights reflected and bounced off the curves of her body. A beautiful, sexually appealing toughness exuded from her and as she shook his hand, his senses immediately felt invigorated and his body stimulated as waves of sexual attraction flooded into every ounce of his existence. Jonas felt alive in a way he'd never felt before.

"I'm Alivia." She remarked with a deep, seductive, rich tone her words melted into Jonas's ears as she spoke. "Nice to meet you."

A temptation now presented itself to Jonas, whether he should indulge and engage in further conversations and interactions with this alluring female or whether he should abstain. Technically he contemplated, it wouldn't actually be cheating on anyone as Martine hadn't yet indicated a romantic interest in him and they'd only been out alone together a couple times. His thoughts wavered for a moment longer with uncertainty as he glanced at Alivia once more. Flirting with this sexually enticing female was not actually breaching any relationship rules he finally concluded as he succumbed to his physical desires and decided to participate fully in whatever kinds of interactions she wanted to engage in.

Corbin's presence had totally disintegrated into the background by now and had become totally irrelevant to Jonas. He perhaps sensed this as he disappeared from the lounge, though no one present actually noticed his departure. Alivia and Jonas were now locked into their conversation and had now been left alone free to explore their introduction in whichever manner they chose too.

"How long have you been a client of Prohuman?" Jonas ventured to ask as he attempted to make as much small talk as possible anxious to secure and retain her attention.

The leather strap outfit she wore was black and almost warrior like, giving her the appearance of an Amazonian princess. Her bronze skin looked oiled slightly as it glimmered and shone and Jonas mouth watered as admired it. He caught a glance of her succulent thighs as she strode back towards a nearby sofa and the flaps of the leather skirt she wore raised slightly and exposed them. He breathed in deeply and intensely as he watched her frozen on the spot as his body was seized and paralyzed by absolute sexual captivation. Right now, Jonas was indeed a hostage to his sexual arousal and he was fully willing to surrender and succumb to that.

"I joined a few months ago." She remarked as she motioned to him to join her on the sofa.

Alivia smiled and he shook himself out of his frozen state and eagerly participated as he sat down very close to her. She moved even closer to him and he held his breath as thoughts tumbled through his mind and his heart beat raced in his chest. Jonas couldn't believe his luck as he ventured to consider and indulge the possibility that this beautiful, sexually alluring female was actually hitting on him. For a moment he was unsure. Nervously he finally decided that perhaps he was reading too much into the situation and that she was probably just being friendly as he attempted to control the feelings of sexual desire that were starting to overwhelm him.

"I'm just about to participate in my first challenge." Jonas remarked as he tried anxiously to steer the conversation away from anything that could possibly arouse him further. "I just signed up this week."

"If you like I can join you and show you the ropes." She offered.

Jonas swallowed a little nervously. His attraction to her was becoming stronger now and he was becoming more and more aroused as each second passed. He wasn't sure he'd be strong enough to contain his desires for her whilst spending time with her for very much longer. He'd have to be strong, he concluded as he decided to accept her invitation. If he refused her invitation he knew there was a possibility that he would not be presented with such an opportunity again and the desire to see what would manifest between them by participating overpowered him as he accepted her offer.

"That would be great." He replied, a huskiness laced his voice that betrayed him and exposed his sexual arousal.

Whether Alivia noticed the change of tone in his voice or not soon became irrelevant however as she stood up a few seconds later, took his hand and led him gently to a capsule nearby.

"Let's go to my capsule." She suggested. "I have a lot more access to Recreation than you do."

Jonas nodded as they entered inside her capsule, his mind fixated and captivated by every swing of her hips as she walked a step or two in front of him. Her tiny waist, pert backside and shapely, succulent hips gave her body voluptuous curves that he was powerless to resist.

Once inside Alivia closed the capsule door and they stood by the control pedestal which arose from the ground as a menu appeared on the capsule wall in front of them displaying several options:

- Attacker challenges.
- Recreation.
- Skill Building.

Alivia smiled and touched the Recreation option, without even consulting Jonas about her choice.

"You don't have this option yet on your menu." She explained. "I want to show you what you can do within this part of the system. You have to get quite a few rewards before you can unlock it."

He nodded in agreement, understanding and accepting her explanation as he appreciated her thoughtfulness.

Suddenly a large skateboard appeared before them in the middle of a grey street as the walls of the capsule evaporated around them. Alivia jumped onto it energetically and grabbed Jonas's hand as she led him. He followed her onto the skateboard as it began to move rapidly down the street. Jonas found himself rocking backwards and forwards as he tried to maintain his balance and steady himself.

Alivia giggled at his obvious struggle and grabbed his hands she placed them firmly on her hips and pulled him closer towards her. Jonas held his breath as he started to feel strong surges of passion stir within him.

"Don't be scared Jonas, you can come a little closer." She teased playfully.

Jonas was exasperated, did this woman actually have no idea what kind of feelings she was evoking inside him, he contemplated. Perhaps she was teasing him intentionally he considered. He thought a little more about whether or not she actually had any notion of just how attractive she really was to him and how sexually aroused her presence alone made him feel. His struggle to control his arousal was intensifying and he had no idea how much longer he could resist the sexual urges he felt inside him. He couldn't pull himself away, there was nowhere to go and Jonas knew he was almost reaching the point of no return, where he'd have to act and fulfill his desires one way or another.

The skateboard journey continued as they flew up the sides of walls, jumped over huge spaces and rode through tunnels. Jonas was no longer paying any attention to his surroundings or the skateboard however as his eyes and mind became totally fixated on Alivia's body and he yearned and longed to be inside her.

Eventually the skateboard journey came to an end and Jonas sighed with relief as they arrived back inside Alivia's capsule. The skateboard now vanished but he was unable to release his grip on her hips as his hands lingered, unwilling to let them go. Alivia stepped back against him and pressed her body up against his. Jonas could no longer resist and for him this was the invitation and clarification he'd been waiting for he needed no further prompting. He immediately started to kiss her passionately and touch her, slipping his hands inside her sparse leather clothing. Alivia groaned with pleasure as she reciprocated. He lifted the flaps of her skirt from behind and penetrated her as she moaned with sexual pleasure and excitement.

Jonas lunged inside her, no longer held back by his rational thoughts and attempts to control his physical desires, no longer burdened by contemplations surrounding his romantic interest in Martine as his body pounded against Alivia's. He satisfied himself relatively quickly due to the fact the sexual tension had been mounting inside him for a couple of hours but he still yearned for more.

Alivia indulged him as she turned to face him and knelt down in front of him. At that moment Jonas knew thoughts of a possibile of a romantic relationship with Martine were instantly over. There was absolutely no way Martine's pretty face and wholesome character could even compete or compare with this immensely, sexually attractive female, who had claimed him as her own from the first minute she'd laid eyes on him.

Alivia smiled as she started to orally pleasure him, Jonas closed his eyes and started to enjoy the intense sexual pleasure she was unleashing onto his physical body. He knew absolutely nothing about this woman but right at this moment in time, it absolutely didn't matter to him and he knew it. Whatever her situation was and whatever the reality of her life was, he knew instantly he was willing to accept her as her sexual power cast its web over him and she ensnared him.

Less than an hour later as Jonas prepared to leave Recreation, fully sexually satisfied, he turned to face Alivia and smiled. He'd had a great baptism into the joys of Recreation and some of the intrigue and delights it could possibly offer him. He looked at her silently for a moment deep in thought as she smiled back at him.

"Is what we did real?" Jonas then proceeded to ask her curiously breaking the silent pause between them. "I mean we had sex right, but we didn't I guess."

Alivia smiled.

"It's as real as you want to make it Jonas." She replied enticingly.

Jonas smiled, pleased by her response. He'd enjoyed their interaction but his body now longed to make it real, he longed to feel the warmth of satisfying her in reality and he was hopeful she would oblige, participate and fulfill that desire.

The next morning Jonas awoke bright and early and decided to actually call Alivia. The phone rang and as he waited eagerly for her to answer it he suddenly became very aware of how strange it was too have had such a powerful, sexually fulfilling liaison with a woman he knew nothing about and had never actually even met in person. It was strange but alluring, weird somehow but extremely wonderful, captivating and exciting.

A few seconds later Alivia answered his call and broke into his thoughts as she disturbed and interrupted them. Her voice on the phone was pleasant and sounded almost the same as it had inside Recreation which please Jonas instantly. He suddenly felt grateful that something in reality was already matching up the unreal experience they'd already enjoyed. Jonas was aware that their physical appearance in Recreation differed slightly from their actual physical appearance in real life and he hoped that neither of them would feel disappointed when they actually met face to face by each other's physical realities. He attempted to catch up in reality with the interactions they'd had in Recreation, the artificial virtual environment they'd engaged in as they engaged in further discussion.

"What do you do for a living?" Jonas ventured to ask, acutely aware that he knew absolutely nothing about this woman.

"I'm a cosmetic surgeon." She replied.

They continued to make small talk for a while though Jonas didn't even touch on the topic of what had actually transpired between them the previous night and stayed miles away from it slightly scared to approach it. It seemed awkward to discuss and Jonas avoided it, Alivia seemed to also and not a word was uttered about it between them. He was eager to organize a real life date with her as he imagined how much he might enjoy real life sexual intimacy between them. Jonas was hopeful that when it actually happened in real life that it would live up to his expectations and the night of passion they'd already shared.

"Can we meet tomorrow?" Jonas asked politely, anxious to meet her as soon as he possibly could in order to establish and seal their sexual bond further with social and romantic interactions.

There was a pause for a second and Jonas started to panic as he wondered how he would feel if she actually rejected him and refused to meet him or how he'd accept the situation if it transpired she was married or unavailable. He coughed to clear his throat nervously as he waited for her response. Alivia sensed his urgency and uncertainty almost instantly, she understood his desire to realize their meeting in reality but like Jonas she was also filled with feelings of nervousness, worried that their meeting may not live up to their initial passionate experience together. Could reality be adjourned and postponed through uncertainty or would that simply creating a more unbearable curiosity that would plague them both. The question danced within her thoughts and teased her as she prepared to respond.

Alivia agreed to meet and put Jonas at ease once more as his doubts and fears of rejection evaporated and disappeared leaving him feeling relieved and validated. They began to make plans for their physical meeting the next day.

"What time would you like to meet?" Alivia asked. "I'm available all day tomorrow." She volunteered.

Jonas smiled enthusiastically, relieved that their first meeting would take place soon and suggested a meeting place that was situated in the center of town. Now in Jonas's mind the only question that remained to be answered was if Alivia would be so forward and willing as she had been inside Recreation, in a real life setting. He yearned for a real realization of their sexual chemistry and he started to prepare mentally for the possibility that it may indeed happen the very next day.

Their conversation ended a few minutes later and Jonas suddenly realized, up until now he hadn't actually done anything or spent any time within Recreation on his own. He shrugged the thoughts from his mind a few seconds later however, satisfied that his liaison with Alivia had been more enjoyable for now than perhaps attacking the various different targets Recreation allocated to his Clan for their attack tasks. Those activities he decided could wait for another day and time, for now he thought right now he had much more pressing matters to attend to. Real sexual fulfillment was now calling to him and his body yearned to materialize his sexual experience with Alivia in reality as the lure of tantalizing sexual intertwining's beckoned to him and started to capture his thoughts, occupy the passageways of his mind and engage his emotions. His mind became totally engrossed as his thoughts filled with Alivia throughout the day and left little space for other non-essential contemplations. His actions became mechanical as he carried out his daily routine tasks. Jonas was now brimming over with eager anticipation, he disguised and contained his excitement however as he stumbled through the rest of the day's events, paying very little attention to them or those surrounding him.

He had attended work that day but was very distracted and detached. The urging inside him pleaded with the day to end and the next morning to arrive as quickly as possible. The next day was one of his days off and he intended to spend as much off it as he could with Alivia. Jonas was hopeful that his eagerness would be rewarded the next day with the real physical, intimate experience he craved and longed for.

Martine called Jonas later that evening but they only spoke for a few minutes. She sensed almost immediately that he seemed distracted and distant and the conversation ended very quickly. She pondered for a few moments as to the possible reason for his distance as the call ended.

Martine placed her phone back down on the table beside her, a little confused by his sudden detachment and the obvious lack of interest in the conversation she'd attempted to hold with him. She started to speculate as she wondered if perhaps he'd lost interest in her or possibly met someone else. After all Martine knew she hadn't really encouraged him or given him any kind of reassurances that she was even particularly interested in him in a romantic sense. Perhaps she thought he'd been enticed by someone else who'd been more clear about their romantic interest in him and he'd been swayed to participate by mutual attraction. There was no commitment between them and Martine knew that she had not been particularly anxious to make one.

Martine resigned herself to the possibility she now faced that Jonas was now probably losing interest in her and that he was making it obvious. She quickly reminded herself once more of Ray Raskal, he was still on her radar, albeit that he'd slipped into the background more recently due to her interactions with Jonas. His position in the background however was not a permanent one and she knew she could always restore him to his rightful place at the forefront of her romantic landscape once more if she so desired. Ray Raskal would require a little more effort on her part however as he had displayed absolutely no signs of romantic interest in her at all. The possibility of romance between them however was now a matter that she needed to explore more fully, Martine decided as she concluded that Jonas's pursuit was now in decline. The time was right she concluded to make Ray Raskal a priority.

The next day as Jonas prepared to meet Alivia with eagerness, he speculated excitedly as he prepared for the possible outcomes of the evening ahead. Though his mind was filled with intense sexual desires, a small part of him attempted to keep his emotions and inner sexual turmoil calm, after all he knew in reality that nothing sexual might actually happen that night at all. Jonas thought further about Alivia's boldness on their first meeting inside Recreation and started to speculate that her boldness in that artificial virtual environment may not match her actions, personality and behavior in real life. People often did things in false environments and situations that they would never even dream of doing in real life. Jonas knew he had to keep that thought at the forefront of his mind and control his excitement, he had no desire to end their first real evening together disappointed or frustrated.

The restaurant they met in was quiet as the waitress showed them to a table in an alcove towards the rear of the venue. Alivia looked stunning and her skin which looked olive now and not bronze as it had appeared inside Recreation, shimmered and shone as the dim lights inside the room reflected upon her face and exposed arms. She looked extremely elegant dressed in a soft, white and gold, clinging pencil dress and Jonas was very content and pleased by the reality of her appearance. They placed their orders and the waiter departed. Once they were alone Alivia leaned forward and whispered in his ear to share a few humorous thoughts regarding the restaurant's menu that she'd observed. Jonas smiled in response as he touched her hand, his mind internally flooded with sexual visions from the moments of intimacy they'd already shared. His touch was an attempt on his part to validate that she was happy with his real physical appearance but she didn't respond, leaving the question in his mind unanswered and the reality impossible to determine. It was impossible for Jonas to draw a conclusion and he finally abandoned the search for validation and certainty as he began to focus on the food, wine and music instead.

Their meeting and meal was slightly awkward for the first thirty minutes. Jonas couldn't determine whether he should flirt with her sexually and be flamboyant or whether he should approach her a little more carefully. He realized they had actually spent very little time together in real life the dilemma that confused him proved it. If they understood each other more, he knew he'd have known exactly what to do and what Alivia would be comfortable with. He finally decided not to rush anything. He was a little stiff and had masked the uncertainty and deliberations that jumped around in his mind as he smiled, made small talk and listened to Alivia his outward appearance seemingly fully attentive and focused.

The wine helped them both to relax a little as the evening progressed; they ate, drank and soon

Jonas found they were both starting to unwind and relax naturally. The relaxation induced by the wine allowed them to overcome any awkwardness between them as they started to appreciate and enjoy each other's company more fully as Alivia shared more details with him about her life and they continued to converse. The dilemma in Jonas's mind as the evening drew on, scampered out of his thoughts and totally disappeared like a rabbit in the woods bounding down a path towards its hole, hidden in the ground.

An hour later once the meal had ended, they headed towards their cars parked nearby. Alivia invited Jonas too her home.

"Let's go to mine." Alivia boldly suggested as they left the restaurant as she giggled.

Jonas was filled with excited and hope as he nodded enthusiastically, they entered inside his car and made their way to her apartment. He opted for automatic drive as he typed in her address and put his arm around her. He decided he wanted to try to make the most of time available to him and throughout the journey to her home, he focused his attention fully on Alivia as he attempted to lubricate and usher in intimacy between them.

Alivia by now was quite tipsy n due to the wine they had consumed and succumbed eagerly and easily as she yielded to his touch. She wasn't quite as forward with him as she had been the first night they'd met inside Recreation but as he touched the inside of her blouse and caressed her breasts with his hands, she giggled with delight which encouraged him.

Jonas started to conclude that the night ahead might not be as totally exciting as the initial experience he'd had with her the previous night within Recreation. In real life she definitely wasn't as bold, sexually assertive or confident as she'd been inside Recreation but he appeased himself with the thought as they drew closer to her home that this time whatever manifest between them would actually be real. The reality aroused him sufficiently enough to forget the expectations of wild passion and satisfy himself with what Alivia was actually comfortable enough to indulge in..

Thoughts of Martine entered his mind for a split second as he felt a slight pang of guilt but he quickly dismissed them. He now had a woman in front of him that was sexually willing, able and participating. Three things which Martine had never been. Even after drinking a couple of bottles of wine during the evening they'd actually spent together, he hadn't felt comfortable enough to attempt to hold her hand, let alone invite her to his home and she'd definitely made no attempts to invite him to hers.

Once inside Alivia's home, Jonas grasped at her body passionately. His passion was still driven by reminders of the images that burned in his mind from the prior encounter they'd experienced as he reflected upon them and his mind filled with visions of them making love inside Recreation. He had every intention to make this night as similar as he could in terms of the experience he'd already enjoyed.

Alivia participated and welcomed him and as he lifted her up onto the kitchen worktop nearby, pushed up her skirt and penetrated her, she groaned and moaned with pleasure.

A few hours later as they lay together in her bedroom he looked at her as she slept. They'd had sex twice before she'd finally fallen asleep exhausted and worn out. Jonas was satisfied that he'd satisfied her. The sexual experience for him hadn't been as mind blowing as he'd hoped it would be, his expectations he knew however were unrealistically rather high due to their artificial sexual interactions inside Recreation.

Jonas considered the future and thought that as they met more often Alivia would become more comfortable with him and it was possible that their sexual experiences together may eventually match and even exceed the initial enjoyment they'd shared as they explored their darkest sexual desires and passions with each other. He yearned for her to display the unbridled passion he'd seen burning in her eyes within Recreation that first night, where she'd cast off her inhibitions and her sexual prowess had run wild and free.

In real life Jonas had found Alivia to be a slightly more subdued, quieter, milder version of the woman he'd met inside Recreation which had disappointed him slightly. He hoped that this would change at a later point in time and he warmed himself with the glimmer of hope that she would relax with him and that one day soon it would. He longed for her one day to become the Alivia he'd met in Recreation though part of him knew that this desire in reality may never actually be fully realized.

Jonas's mind began to wander as he speculated further unable to sleep as Alivia lay in his arms if it was only in dreams and an unreal state that human beings sexual desires, fantasies and sexual liberation could ever be fully realized.

He continued to contemplate, deliberate and speculate over these thoughts as finally sleep crept into the bed around him, coated his skin and carried him off into the night; he drifted and floated away peacefully into the realms of his dreams as the night embraced him.

INSIDE THE PLAYGROUND

Jonas found a free slot in his schedule a week later and he dedicated it to exploring Recreation more fully. He'd started to spend a lot of his free time with Alivia but due to work commitments he now found he had only a handful of hours here and there to enjoy in any way he wished too. He'd decided to allocate some of this time to exploring his Recreation subscription and to actually participate in some of the Attacker activities his clan group were supposed to engage in.

One evening, the perfect opportunity arose as he found himself alone, without any work or social commitments and with nothing to do. He sat on the sofa in the lounge and put on his headset as he prepared to access Recreation. He switched it on and immediately found himself in the Attacker's lounge.

Jonas gazed around as he entered inside, the Black sofa's in the Attacker's lounge lay empty and there were no other Recreation participants visible to him. He made his way towards his capsule and entered inside. The menu screen appeared on the capsule walls in front of him as the door of the capsule closed behind him. The control stick immediately rose up from the floor from where it was concealed, a thin gear stick type object with a pad situated on the top with various buttons you could press. Jonas also knew however that you could also touch the walls of the capsule to select preferences from the various menus they displayed and as his options appeared on the wall in front of him, he selected the 'Attacker Challenges' option, from the next menu that appeared he then selected 'Attack A Target' from the next menu that appeared in front of him.

A street suddenly appeared all around him as the walls of the capsule disappeared, the buildings within it were all different colors and the walls of the buildings were made up off people. A map appeared in one corner of the wall with a red building on it. Twenty people all dressed in red, with red skin and hair were situated in the walls of the building that was highlighted as his target. Jonas concluded that he had to run through the streets, locate the building and avoid all the attacks and flying objects along the way as he prepared to set off on his mission.

Jonas smiled as he started to duck, dive and weave, he rolled over the ground, ran across roads and darted behind walls whilst making his way steadily towards the building. Throughout the journey he made he was attacked by flying objects that shot out of the buildings nearby and headed straight for him like missiles. He ran up the walls of buildings, jumped from ledges and jumped across rooftops until about fifteen minutes later he finally reached his target destination.

Once he arrived at the building he paused unsure for a moment about what he was actually supposed to do next. He touched the control pad for a moment and a program suddenly appeared next to him all dressed in black with black shiny hair and jet black skin.

"I'm Destroyer your program guide." Destroyer remarked as he introduced himself to Jonas. "I see you've reached your target."

Jonas nodded.

"OK. I'll show you how to destroy them." Destroyer replied. "Once you destroy the target all the people in the walls of the building become your foot soldiers. Whilst you are away from Recreation they conduct Missions for you. When you attend Attacker challenges in future you can also bring them along with you on the mission to assist."

Jonas looked at the people in the walls of the building nearby curiously for a moment.

"Are they real people?" He asked curiously.

Destroyer shook his head.

"They're just program simulations. You can't interact with them, only command them." Destroyer replied. "You can however build an army with them. They become your Foot Soldiers, once you conquer the building they resided in."

Jonas nodded in understanding as Destroyer led him towards the target building. They made their way around the exterior planting bombs around the walls. On one occasion they were attacked by a Guard and Destroyer taught Jonas how to physically fight with the Building Guards. Once they were overpowered they submitted and once they submitted they disappeared evaporating into nothingness.

"There are usually a few Building Guards scattered around any building you attack. Once you overpower them however they disappear." Destroyer explained. "Your real major threat is Protectors. If a Protector is guarding a target and they attack you, they can destroy your army of foot soldiers and deplete members any army you've built."

Jonas nodded as he listened.

Destroyer grabbed his arm and they ran down the street to a nearby alleyway and hid. They peeked out from behind the wall that concealed them every few seconds as they watched the target building intently. Destroyer brought out a detonator from underneath one of his leather straps where it had been hidden and pressed it. The target building blew up a few seconds later. Jonas watched from the corner of the alleyway as the people and debris from the building flew into the air and spread out all over the street nearby. Destroyer smiled and ran back out of the alleyway as Jonas followed him.

They made their way back towards the street where the target building had been situated but now there only debris remained strewn across the street in front of them. Destroyer started to run around the building and as he ran into the colored foot soldiers that now lay scattered around on the street, Jonas noticed he was collecting them. Once he finished he stood next to Jonas and smiled.

"The target is destroyed and you now have twenty foot soldiers." He remarked.

Jonas nodded appreciatively.

"Thanks for showing me how to destroy a target." He replied.

Destroyer smiled.

"Anytime you need assistance just access the menus and select Program Guide Assistance and I'll appear immediately to assist you." Destroyer explained.

Jonas nodded.

Inside Jonas felt good as the street suddenly disappeared around him and he returned once more to his capsule. He'd collected twenty foot soldiers and had successfully completed his first Attacker Clan mission. He was now a fully-fledged Attacker Clan Member. Though the mission hadn't been as exhilarating as his interaction with Alivia that first evening he'd accessed Recreation, it had still been fun. He now understood the missions within his range of clan activities and how he could build his empire.

A few weeks had passed since Martine's initial realization that Jonas's interest in her and attention was beginning to wane; it was becoming increasingly obvious to her that things were cooling off between them and she was almost sure now he was seeing someone else. Their phone conversations had became shorter and shorter and his calls were less frequent and now actually quite rare. She began to feel it was almost as if he only called her nowadays out of courtesy, more than a desire to communicate and strengthen their emotional bond. Martine decided to move on fully and started to engineer her plan to meet Ray Raskal in a way that would capture his attention. Her plan sought clarification one way or another as to whether Ray Raskal was remotely interested in her romantically and whether the possibility of a romance between could ever actually happen.

Martine decided to concoct a situation that may allow her to establish this and almost as if fate was listening and conspiring to assist her, additional circumstances started to lend a hand. That week as she attempted to facilitate her headset to enter Recreation, she began to receive some very strange error messages. Instead of notifying the program guides as she knew she could do, she decided instead to utilize the opportunity to attempt to meet Ray Raskal and visit Prohuman HQ in person.

Martine prepared as she dressed in an elegant, figure hugging, mid-thigh length black dress, she allowed her hair to fall down and flow out across her shoulders decorating her frame with ringlets and locks as it spread out, the dark locks embracing her neck and framing her face. She picked up a pair of black, strappy heels and put them on. Inside she had absolutely no misgivings about what she was doing, she was seeking clarity and fulfillment of her deepest sexual desires for a man she was very attracted to. Desires she'd suppressed, ignored and rejected up until now due to the presence of Jonas in her life. Now that his presence was evaporating into the background, Martine was now free and anxious to explore more deeply her attraction to Ray Raskal.

Arriving inside the reception an hour later a male receptionist greeted Martine cheerfully. He wore a badge on his shirt that read Jaylon.

"How can I assist you?" Jaylon asked politely as he walked out from behind the majestic black, shiny, marble desk that Martine had admired on her initial visit.

"I'm having a problem with the system. I'm receiving funny error messages whenever I enter into my capsule." Martine explained, she hesitated for a moment before she continued, "I haven't done anything unusual or different so I'm not sure why."

Jaylon walked back towards the marble reception desk nearby and beckoned towards Martine to follow him. She walked over towards him and stood at the other side of the desk politely waiting as Jaylon touched a screen situated upon it and looked at it for a few minutes intensely. He was engrossed in his task and after a slight pause that lasted a few minutes, he finally looked up at her once more and smiled.

"Take a seat on one of the sofa's I've notified a coordinator and they're on their way." He insisted as he waved his arm towards one of the plush, black leather sofas that lined the walls of the reception area.

Martine thanked him and made her way over to the nearest sofa and sat down. A few minutes later a young man in his mid-twenties showed up and Jaylon looked at him as he entered through the glass doors from one of the nearby hallways.

"Trystan you're here, great as per my email, our client is experiencing some problems when she accesses Recreation." Jaylon remarked as he entered the foyer.

Jaylon nodded towards Martine and Trystan made his way over towards her enthusiastically as he smiled to greet her.

"If you'd like to come with me please." He remarked.

Martine smiled and stood up obligingly as she accepted his offer of assistance as he led her back through the glass doorway he'd just emerged from. Trystan politely held the door open, allowed her to enter inside and then followed her into the hallway. They walked down the hallway and he started to make polite conversation with her as they walked which instantly put Martine at ease.

"How are you enjoying the Prohuman experience so far?" He enquired politely.

"Oh it's wonderful." Martine replied as she nodded enthusiastically. "Very intriguing and enjoyable. I've also met a lot of interesting people. I've even been rewarded with some enhanced skills that widen my access, capacity and capabilities now, it's very exciting."

"Great we like our customers to feel satisfied." Trystan remarked. "It makes our job much more enjoyable too."

Martine continued to lag a step or two behind him as he led her towards a white door at the bottom of the hallway.

"We don't often have customer complaints and system errors." Trystan explained. "So this is a very unusual situation."

Martine nodded in understanding as he touched a fingerprint pad beside the doorway to verify his fingerprint and identity. A few seconds later the door in front of them slid open. He beckoned towards Martine to follow him as they entered inside.

Inside the doorway was another hallway and as they walked down it Martine started to feel a little nervous. She realized now she was obviously in a secure area of Prohuman headquarters and for a moment she was unsure exactly what would happen next. She contemplated what may possibly occur, would Ray Raskal be situated where they were going or would it simply be engineers and support technicians who actually fixed the system errors. Once they were fixed would they simply dismiss her and send her home? She quickly began to realize that this visit may not even provide her with the meeting opportunity with Ray Raskal at all she'd initially hoped for.

Trystan led her into a room at the end of the hallway, it was a huge space with lots of systems and a huge screen grid on one wall with lots of orange and blue bright lights dotted all over it. The dots as Martine peered at the screen, she observed were collated into five main areas which almost looked like countries or lands on a map.

Two engineers were seated in front of the wall focused on watching the array of lights in front of them. When Martine and Trystan entered their attention turned towards them for a moment as they looked at them curiously, they looked surprised by their appearance. Trystan led Martine towards one of the engineers nearby and started to introduce them to each other.

"These are some of our system engineers, this is Enoch and that's Bexley." Trystan explained as he headed towards Bexley, internally he'd already decided she would be the most helpful in this situation.

"What are all those lights?" Martine asked him curiously as she continued to follow him.

Trystan smiled and gazed at the large screen on the wall for a moment before he replied.

"Ah those represent active users within Recreation at any given moment in time." He explained.

Bexley an Asian female with light brown skin and dark short hair, smiled at Martine as they approached and Martine instantly felt at ease.

"If you like I can show you how we monitor the system." Bexley offered as she assumed that Martine was some kind of special guest that Trystan was showing around, anxious to be as helpful as possible she volunteered to assist them immediately.

Martine nodded intrigued and filled with curiosity as Bexley offered her a seat nearby and she sat down beside her. Bexley handed her a headset and she put it on as Bexley touched one of the orange dots on the screen in front of them.

Immediately Martine could see an outdoor area where a user was engaging in a challenge. The user a female in her thirties was riding a dark, coal colored horse. Martine smiled as the female user approached a pile of wooden logs that the horse was supposed to jump over. The horse stopped abruptly in front of the pile of logs and pulled its head down rapidly towards the ground. The female rider fell off the back of the horse as she landed on the ground nearby. Surprised by the horse's actions, she'd lost her balance almost immediately and Martine smiled as she watched.

Bexley touched another dot and Martine now found herself watching ten people inside a nightclub as they danced on the dance floor together. She watched them silently for a few moments before Bexley touched the screen once more, Martine now found herself watching two people sliding down a water ride at the Recreation Theme Park.

"At any moment in time we can monitor who is doing what anywhere in the system if we need to. We don't tend to however unless there is a problem that needs to be fixed." Bexley explained. "We tend to feel it's a bit intrusive to spy on people for no reason."

Martine nodded accepting and understanding the logic behind Bexley's explanation.

"Now let me show you something a little more unusual." Bexley continued.

Bexley touched a corner of the screen and Martine suddenly found herself in a corridor with bright lights flooding the area around her. Binary codes then appeared all around her that glowed and shone. A few seconds later the codes and bright lights melted away almost as if she'd passed through a wormhole of some kind and Martine found herself standing alone in a large black space.

Boxes started to appear before her creating a wall nearby, their sudden appearance broke the intensity of the black expanse which had initially appeared to Martine be infinite. Numerous words were etched on the boxes which shone and illuminated as Martine paused for a moment unsure what she was supposed to do next. She stared at the wall in front of her motionless and frozen for a few seconds before Bexley interrupted her.

"Touch one." Bexley urged as she encouraged her to interact with the environment she was situated in.

Bexley had sensed Martine's hesitation and attempted to provide clarity in response. Martine nodded in agreement and stretched a hand forward as she touched the box that read 'Sea Challenges', she then quickly took a few steps backwards. Martine watched for a few seconds tentatively unsure as she waited to see what would happen next. A few seconds later he curiosity was answered as she was sucked into an area with a golden sand beach and coral reefs the aqua sea that surrounded it was peaceful and the waves nearby lapped gently against the shore on which she stood. Scuba equipment lay strewn on the golden, honey colored sand nearby and she smiled in awe as she fully absorbed the beauty of her surroundings.

"This is where people engage in some sea challenges." Bexley explained. "We can access all the various challenge areas from this part of the system to test and refine them." She remarked. "Our jobs can actually be quite fun sometimes as we get to try out all the new features in the system first."

Martine nodded as she switched off the headset, the beach faded immediately as it evaporated into sudden nonexistence in front of her very eyes. She removed the headset and turned once more to face Bexley as she smiled. Martine handed the headset back to her and Bexley smiled. Bexley then paused as she held it for a few seconds, she gazed into the air deep in thought for a moment then turned to look at Martine and Trystan once more curiously.

"What else can I do for you both?" Bexley asked as the realization struck her that she didn't actually know why Martine had even been brought to the engineering room by Trystan in the first place.

Trystan started to explain as he smiled at her.

"Martine is having some problems with the system, she's experiencing some error messages." He explained.

Martine nodded in agreement to verify that was indeed why she was there. Bexley moved across the room to a smaller screen situated at a computer nearby and motioned towards Martine to join her.

"What's your user name?" Bexley asked as she touched the screen and entered some commands.

"Martinique." Martine replied.

Bexley nodded and continued to access more menus and touch more options on the screen. She quickly found Martine's profile and her body image and profile details appeared in front of them as she watched. Bexley nodded towards her as she noticed a message flash at the bottom of the screen and touched it to access more information. The error message she touched prompted another screen to load and a list of ten messages suddenly appeared in front of them.

"I see what the problem is." Bexley explained as she read the list and turned once more to face Martine once more. "I'll have it fixed straight away. The error messages should be gone the next time you access Recreation." She insisted reassuringly.

The doorway of the engineering control room suddenly slid open and Athena swept in as everyone turned to face her abruptly. She looked at Martine strangely for a moment, then turned to face Trystan and Bexley. Athena now stood frozen and motionless as she looked at them intensely for a few seconds. They immediately fell silent as they looked at her, like naughty schoolchildren caught with their hands in the cookie jar. A second later she swept briskly across the room towards them.

"What is she doing in here?" She snapped abruptly at Trystan and Bexley as Athena pointed towards Martine.

Martine started to feel nervous and uncomfortable she immediately sensing Athena's agitation from the tone in her voice. Everyone could sense the tension in the air as Trystan and Bexley looked at each other, unsure how to respond.

"You shouldn't be in here." Athena started to explain to Martine in a slightly softer tone as she realized suddenly that she'd scared her.

The expression on Martine's face was by now one of total horror as she wished the walls of the room would absorb her and she could melt inside of them.

Trystan instantly stood up as if to defend her and started to explain apologetically. "Sorry Athena I brought her here. I thought if I brought her down here the engineers could fix the problems and error messages she was experiencing straight away."

"We'll discuss this later Trystan." Athena barked as she looked at Trystan with an expression of utter distaste, her words were laced with tones that clearly illustrated her anger and upset.

Trystan flinched at her tone as he realized this was not going to be dismissed as a simple mistake and he may be possibly be disciplined for what he'd done. He swallowed nervously as he stood for a moment frozen and unsure what to do next.

"Trystan will accompany you back to the reception." Athena continued as she smiled at Martine somewhat artificially though she was seething inside she quickly made a weak attempt to reassure her that things were fine. "It's not your fault, Trystan really shouldn't have brought you down here."

Athena's blood by now was at boiling point and it simmered below her skin like the liquid pot simmered on the searing heat of a stove. Her temper flared and so did her nostrils as she attempted to control herself. She was livid but the thought that Martine was a paying client and that an angry outburst in front of her was not a desirable situation, restrained her reaction. She would however she decided once she was back in her office make a note on Trystan's personnel file about his failure to follow the internal Prohuman Inc. procedures. Athena was irritated by his conduct, the staff procedure manual was very clear and clients were not allowed any access to the secure areas of Prohuman headquarters in any situation. The engineering control room was one of the four secure areas and he'd directly disobeyed the instructions in the employee procedural manual. Trystan had breached these procedures and had even done so in front of other staff, this was an issue she knew she would have to deal with at a later date more formally.

Trystan nodded nervously towards Martine as he started to lead her out of the engineering control room and back down the nearby corridor they'd entered from.

"I'm very sorry." Martine remarked quietly as they walked. "I didn't mean to get you in any kind of trouble."

Trystan shook his head.

"It's totally not your fault." He insisted. "Athena's just strict sometimes unnecessarily. We were just unlucky to catch her on a bad day. Usually she's not so regimental, sometimes she's actually even quite nice." He remarked. "Maybe she's had an argument with her boyfriend." He said quietly as he smiled mischievously at Martine for a second.

Martine smiled, relieved at his attempt to reassure her that everything would be fine. They arrived at the doorway leading back to the reception a few minutes later and Trystan opened the glass door for her once more as Martine stepped back into the foyer. Ray Raskal suddenly appeared in the reception area from behind a glass door opposite them and as they entered, he smiled at them. Trystan smiled and nodded to acknowledge his presence as Ray Raskal approached them.

"Problem Trystan?" Ray Raskal asked curiously as he wondered as to why Martine was there.

Trystan nodded his head.

"Martine was receiving some error messages. I took her to see one of the engineers who is working to fix it for her at the moment." He explained.

Ray Raskal nodded in response, satisfied with his reply and gazed at Martine thoughtfully for a moment. Martine smiled gently as she gazed into his eyes as she realized this was her moment.

Her moment to determine if there would ever be anything between them.

"Let me take you to the canteen and organize some refreshments and food for you whilst you wait for the problem to be resolved." Ray Raskal offered, anxious to appease and accommodate Martine as he attempted to recompense her somehow for the inconvenience she'd experienced that had prompted her visit. "Trystan can you notify me immediately please once the problem is fixed." Ray Raskal continued.

Trystan nodded in response, somewhat relieved by Ray Raskal's involvement. His involvement Trystan anticipated might save him from the possible scolding Athena was probably planning to inflict at a later point in time for his disobedience. Trystan scurried off back in the direction of the engineer control room relieved as he smiled and nodded with satisfaction.

Ray Raskal led Martine through the nearby glass door which led to the canteen she'd visited on the days of her induction sessions during her initial visits to Prohuman headquarters. Whilst they walked towards the canteen Ray Raskal talked to her in a manner that seemed gentle, open and apologetic.

"I'm very sorry you're experiencing problems with Recreation and a disruption to your services." He remarked as they arrived at the entrance to the canteen and he touched a switch on the wall outside it.

The canteen door swished open in front of them and he motioned towards it as he encouraged Martine to enter inside. Martine smiled and did so willingly as the excitement built within her regarding the prospects of spending some time with Ray Raskal one on one. She could hardly breath as the tingling and anticipation began to flood through every pore of her body.

"It's ok really. I was just passing by the area so I thought I should drop in, in person to let you guys know." Martine explained as she attempted to verify the innocence of her visit.

"Oh you definitely did the right thing." Ray Raskal replied as he showed her to a nearby table and they sat down together.

He motioned to one of the kitchen staff, who peeked out curiously from the kitchen window as they entered inside. Immediately as soon as he noticed Ray Raskal was in attendance and required service, he rushed out from behind where the kitchen was situated to attend to his requirements. Ray Raskal smiled as the canteen staff member approached them eagerly, pleased by his attentiveness.

"Order anything you like." He encouraged Martine. "Jeremy will prepare it for you immediately."

Martine nodded and smiled appreciatively at Jeremy a Caucasian male in his early fifties who was dressed in a blue and white kitchen uniform.

"Mr. Raskal I had no idea you'd be visiting us this afternoon." Jeremy explained as he smoothed down his apron anxiously and hoped that nothing serious was wrong.

"It's a surprise visit." Ray Raskal explained. "Nothing to worry about."

Jeremy nodded as he turned to face Martine for a moment and handed her a menu. Martine accepted the menu graciously and began to look at the items off food it offered.

"Jeremy can I have some Chicken Satay Sticks, a pot of strong black coffee and some Spicy Tiger Prawns." Ray Raskal requested briskly.

Jeremy nodded as he quickly dipped his hand into the pocket situated at the front of his apron. He plucked out and retrieved the small pencil and notepad that he used to take orders and scribbled down Ray Raskal's order down on it quickly, then turned to face Martine once more.

Martine was still deliberating over her selection, carefully contemplating what she should choose. It had to be something that she knew would take a little longer to prepare she decided. Her plan being to intentionally order something more complex to maximize and provide herself with as much time alone with Ray Raskal as she possibly could.

"Can I have some Buffalo Wings please and for main the steak with fries, well done." She finally confirmed after pausing for a few minutes. "Oh and a latte please."

Martine handed the menu back to Jeremy and smiled graciously at him as internally she continued to speculate about whether the chicken casserole would have taken longer to prepare and if perhaps she should have chosen that instead. She thought about it a bit further before she decided that she'd definitely made the right choice. The casserole she'd speculated was probably already prepared and sitting in a pot which they would simply heat for a few minutes before dishing out a serving. The steak she'd asked for however had to be freshly prepared and cooked which she knew would take the kitchen staff at least ten minutes more.

Jeremy scribbled down her order, nodded and then exited abruptly, leaving Martine and Ray Raskal alone once more.

Ray Raskal smiled at Martine as he gazed into her eyes. Martine immediately felt the sexual tension between them mounting inside her as she admired his physical appearance in close proximity. This was the first time she'd ever been alone with him and she intended to savor every single second.

"How long ago did you establish the company Prohuman Inc.?" Martine asked, very aware that she already knew the answer to the question she posed.

When she'd first read the brochure she'd been sent, she'd read about it but she decided to indulge him in any possible small talk she could think off as she attempted to engage and retain Ray Raskal's full attention.

Ray Raskal smiled flattered by her attentiveness, her interest in his work, his personal dedication to it and her interest in him. He was beginning to appreciate the break from his office, it wasn't often he sat down with anyone never mind a client. It was a refreshing break for him from the monotony of his usual daily routine.

He gazed at Martine before he answered as he started to notice that she was very attractive, her cherry red lips, jet black hair and green eyes were strikingly beautiful as they contrasted against each other and appealed to his visual senses.

In that short space of time, Martine had successfully managed to form a connection with him, she had become more than a customer to Ray Raskal now, she'd become a woman and a very attractive one.

"I started the company a few years ago." He explained. "Everyone thought what I was doing was crazy and that what I wanted to do was too adventurous but I persevered. It gives you an amazing sense of satisfaction to see your dreams actually materialize and be realized."

Martine nodded as she gazed into his eyes attentively and wished inside she could say the words to him that were really on her mind. She knew however it wasn't the right time yet and they were still officially in the client zone. Martine decided she needed to wait for a more suitable invitation from him, which she knew may not even happen that day. She didn't dare push their conversation into personal arenas too abruptly, for fear he may withdraw, perhaps sensing her attraction towards him and maybe even realizing the real motivations for her visit. Martine didn't want Ray Raskal to feel as if she was chasing him and she avoided being too forward, delicately as she kept any conversation she made very light.

A few minutes later Jeremy arrived back with the starters and pots of coffee they'd requested. He put them down quietly on the table and then disappeared again as if he didn't wish to interrupt or disturb their conversation as he did so. Ray Raskal smiled as the pots of coffee and starters arrived and rubbed his hands together enthusiastically.

"Feel free to make a start and help yourself to anything you want." He explained as he pushed the three starter dishes into the middle of the table towards her and started to pour some coffee out off one of the coffee pots into a mug nearby.

Martine smiled impressed by his generosity and his positive attitude. Her feelings towards him were growing by the second, he was not only extremely handsome, Ray Raskal was also very considerate. She contemplated for a moment, as she speculated how those characteristics would translate into the bedroom as she wondered if he'd also be a considerate lover.

Martine knew that she would definitely not get the opportunity to discover his bedroom manner today but she felt satisfied that her visit had indeed been successful. Ray Raskal had now provided her with a glimmer of hope in person that there may one day be a possible romance between them, up until this point in time there had only been a fantasy and remote possibility which had no grounding in reality. Now Martine savored the fact that she could enjoy the memory and manifestation of the real intimate interaction that had actually really occurred between them. The real possibilities for the future between them and possible interactions they could engage in, started to materialize and form in Martine's mind as the many pathways and romantic possibilities formed a maze within her thoughts. Martine smiled as they continued to talk and eat as she continued to entertain thoughts about her fantasies with Ray Raskal which could one day really manifest into real romantic experiences.

Martine was quietly satisfied by her trip to Prohuman headquarters. No matter what happened next between them, Ray Raskal now knew who she was and he'd given her some personal attention. Now she existed to him. In some respects her plan was already a success.

VIRUS ATTACKS

Ray Raskal's nightmares unbeknown to him however had only just begun, once the situation with Martine had been resolved, the error messages started to become more frequent and affected other client's accounts. He suspected a competitor was trying to infiltrate Recreation and that they utilized viruses to attack the system. He scanned the security back end as he searched for clues as to how they were gaining access to attack Recreation. He called an emergency meeting immediately in the large board meeting room and all the staff, engineers, customer liaison representatives and security specialists were present. He paced up and down at the front of the room as he anxiously expressed his concerns to them.

"We're under attack. Everyone must be alert at all times, until we have this situation under control. Two hundred client accounts have been affected and we have to try to eliminate the problem immediately." He explained.

All the engineers looked at each other bewildered as he spoke as they speculated internally as to how they could assist. Around fifty employees were in attendance. Haiden the Chief of Security began to stand as Ray Raskal motioned to him to approach the front of the room. Haiden had already been briefed and he started to provide a breakdown and more precise details surrounding the nature of the infiltration to the room of staff that attended the meeting. Everyone in the room listened to him quietly as he spoke.

Haiden a mature man in his late fifties had been working at Prohuman Inc. since its inception. Ray Raskal trusted him implicitly, he was the best in his particular field, hence the reason Ray had pursued him eagerly to secure his employment within the company. He was calm, extremely intelligent and very hard working. His serious nature was respected by all the employees of Prohuman who were well aware that he did not entertain frivolities or participate in semantics. When Haiden spoke everyone listened.

Ray Raskal was relieved he'd hired such a pragmatic and thorough employee in that particular position as the aspect of security was fundamental to Prohuman Inc.'s success or failure. The service offered to clients came at a high price, if Recreation failed to deliver on promises and was riddled with problems, he knew they would ultimately lose income and clients immediately.

Whilst he spoke Ray Raskal contemplated further the possibility of who could be responsible. He had no known enemies that he could think off. He hadn't rocked anyone's boat or disturbed anyone, nor was he directly in competition with anyone else. It was puzzling and strange to him therefore that his company was under attack. Prohuman Inc.'s entertainment portfolio was quite unique, he'd established his own brand, his own market and targeted his own customer group. Yet here he was being attacked by an invisible enemy.

Cora raised her hand as Haiden finished speaking. Ray Raskal nodded towards her to indicate that she should proceed to ask a question if she wished too. Cora his top developer, he'd plucked straight from university as soon as she'd graduated with top honors. She was an exceptional employee, had contributed a lot of popular elements to the Recreation's system and been responsible for a lot of successful development. In return she was highly paid and given lavish benefits. She was in her mid-twenties, quirky, messy and at times even looked a little unkempt. However despite her outward appearance her work was always immaculate and highly organized which satisfied Ray Raskal, after all he knew he wasn't employing her for her looks or her tidiness. Her points were always valid, intelligent and her opinions highly respected and Ray Raskal was anxious to listen to her question, observation or issue. Haiden turned to face her and to attend to her question enthusiastically as he nodded towards her to encourage her to proceed.

"Is there anything we can do to stop it spreading?" Cora asked curiously.

Haiden nodded.

"Yes that's what we're sorting out at the moment." He explained. "We're forming a defense team to focus on isolating the files corrupted by the virus in an attempt to contain it. We'll also be duplicating affected user profiles and switching clients over to them in an attempt to minimize the disruption to client services."

Ray Raskal nodded as he verified Haiden's response.

"Some of you will be asked to stay behind after the meeting today." He remarked. "You'll form part of the defense team. In the meantime for everyone else if you are dealing with customers on a daily basis, our official response to this situation to clients must be unified. You must reassure them by providing the following comment to enquiries and support calls. 'We are aware of the problem and are taking immediate action to resolve it' at this time you are not permitted to say anything else." Ray Raskal explained.

The client liaison representatives around the board room nodded in agreement. The response from the room to the news of the attacks was one of surprise and their lack of questions after the briefing reflected this. Most of the employees hadn't even realized or been aware of the error message situation at all up until now. The situation had however now escalated and the virus attacks had now become a full blown organizational crisis.

Luckily the response and backlash from clients hadn't yet been too severe as the disruption to their services had been minimalized by Haiden and his team, who had acted quickly to contain the problem straight away. Ray Raskal had been monitoring the situation fervently and Athena had managed some of the clients affected by the virus attacks personally in order to keep client complaints somewhat under control.

"Bexley, Cora, Rueben and Brice please stay behind, the rest of you can go." Ray Raskal announced as the meeting drew to a close and the staff were released to return to their usual daily duties.

Athena stood up and prepared to leave, her face displayed an expression of slight dismay. She hadn't been included in the special defense team, selected to respond to and manage the crisis and she felt slightly rejected by Ray Raskal. She swept towards the door quickly, trying to disguise her disappointment as she wondered why she'd been omitted; hadn't he seen her devotion, all the extra hours she worked regularly, the commitment she put into Prohuman Inc. since she joined over two years ago.

Glancing back at him for a moment as she reached the doorway, she noticed he seemed oblivious to her reaction. His omission and rejection of her seemed to be irrelevant to him at that particular moment in time as he engaged in an in-depth discussion with Haiden and the people he'd asked to stay behind. Athena was hurt but she knew deep down inside her there was nothing she could do about it. If she raised it as an issue, she'd seem immature, demanding and irrational. If she didn't her hurt would accumulate as the situation continued and she was left out of more and more confidential meetings and activities.

Athena walked towards her office nearby as she continued to question Ray Raskal's decision in her mind and wonder why she hadn't been selected, somewhat disgusted by her exclusion. Athena realized however as she walked this wasn't just totally about work. Jealousy was beginning to prick her emotions as she contemplated the time Ray Raskal would be spending with the other employees he'd actually chosen. She wondered for a moment if his actions and omission were an indication, that he was becoming less interested in spending time with her than he once was. At one point in time she had been the lifeblood of the organization, the one he turned to with any problem and the one he deliberated over any major decisions with. On her way inside her office, she sighed with dismay as she made her way over to the desk and sank down into the chair behind it. For the first time since she'd joined Prohuman Inc. she began to feel unimportant almost as if her opinion and input was not deemed non-essential and it hurt.

A few minutes later Athena was jolted suddenly out of her self-pity however as an unexpected knock at the door sounded throughout the room and breached the silence of her office interior. Athena's thoughts crashed as she was immediately mentally drawn back into her surroundings with a bump. She shook her head quickly in disbelief as she attempted to handle the emotional hurt she felt and prepared to face the world once more.

"Come in." She called out loudly as she sat up and held her head up high.

The door swished open a few seconds later and Trystan walked in. She gazed at him as he entered, very surprised by his appearance. Just like her Trystan also hadn't been included in the 'problem resolution and defense team' either and for a remote second she wondered if he too was hurt by his exclusion. Trystan smiled enthusiastically as he sat down in the chair situated at the opposite side of her desk and she realized he seemed somewhat less bothered by the rejection and emotionally unaffected.

"What can I do for you Trystan?" Athena asked politely.

Athena had managed to make her peace with Trystan since the incident with Martine which she was somewhat relieved about. Being that she was his line manager and he was usually a reasonably hard working employee; it had been awkward to have an ongoing dispute with him. She also had no desire to make it a long term bone of contention between them as usually his work was beyond reproach.

Ray Raskal had also mentioned the subject too her at one of their meetings and requested that she should not be too harsh with him; due to the unique nature of the situation and the problem that had created it. Obliging Ray Raskal's request, she'd not lectured him too harshly and the matter was now considered dealt with and as far as they were both concerned buried in the past.

Trystan paused for a second uncertain how to respond. He'd noticed Athena leave the board meeting room rather abruptly and he'd sensed her emotional discomfort and the rejection she felt. He hadn't actually come to her office to ask her anything. He'd simply come to try and appease her and engage her in a manner that made her feel useful, respected and valued once more. He sought his mind quickly as he searched for an excuse and reason for his presence.

"I wanted to discuss my career development plan." He finally remarked after a few seconds.

Athena smiled and touched the screen in front of her as she accessed the relevant files, she was motivated but a little confused by his sudden interest in his career development plan.

Career development plans were an internal system she'd created at Prohuman Inc. and she'd prided herself on the implementation of her system. Each of her team members she'd held regular one to one meetings with, where their career development plan would reviewed and amended according to their needs. Up until now it had never been an area however that Trystan had shown much interest in which had often frustrated her. She thought smugly about it further for a moment as she contemplated that perhaps her consistency and dedication to the process was encouraging him to take his plan more seriously.

Meanwhile back in the board meeting room, Ray Raskal and Haiden were still briefing the defense team he was creating.

"We don't know why, we don't know how and we don't know how long these attacks will last." Ray Raskal explained.

Enoch who had left the board room earlier with the other staff had smiled as he'd left at Reuben and grinned at him cheekily, he wasn't envious at all that Reuben had been selected and he hadn't.

"Rather you than me." Enoch had teased whispering quietly in his ear as he exited.

Enoch and Reuben at the current time were working most of their shifts together which meant they spent a lot of time together. This had encouraged them to develop a rapport between them which had been enhanced by their personalities and interactions. Enoch was definitely more social and had managed to develop a friendship with Reuben that Reuben simply didn't have with other staff and he appreciated that.

"I could do with a bit of overtime." Reuben had reassured him in response as he leant over towards him. "It'll come in handy. Olivia and I are saving."

Enoch had nodded, smiled and winked at him as he left the room and Reuben had smiled in response. Ray Raskal had definitely made the right choice between the two of them and they both knew it. Enoch had a very active social life and would have totally resented having to work longer hours than his usual shifts.

Reuben looked around at the group he was now left with in the meeting room, everyone else had already exited. Cora wasn't particularly bothered about social activities therefore the impact of the extra work hours this additional work would require, meant little to her and she smiled at Haiden and Ray Raskal enthusiastically to verify this but he was unsure about Brice however as he hardly knew him. They'd never exchanged more than a few words and usually worked on different shifts. Bexley he knew as he gazed at her would probably be more impacted than anyone else she was a bit more social and sometimes she even went out to after work drinks with other employees of Prohuman Inc. from Client Liaison Services.

Trystan would often come to collect her after shifts from the engineering control room. They would make their way out to collect other staff members from the various other departments, who they'd disappear with as they laughed and discussed the topics of the day together energetically.

"I'm pulling you all off your usual shifts for a while." Ray Raskal explained abruptly as he gazed around the room. "Until we've resolved the problems."

Engineers worked day shifts and evening shifts, they often started at six in the morning and worked until early evening, the evening shifts would then begin and ended at three in the morning. Ray Raskal had designed the shifts to cover the main hours of usage of the Recreation system by clients. The hours between three and six in the morning he'd decided to leave unmanned during the week days. Upon monitoring the system he'd found very little client facilitation between those hours which had led him to the decision that it wasn't worth allocating labor to them. Throughout the weekends however engineers worked twenty four hours a day due to the fact that many more people had much more leisure time on the weekends to access the system and did so. On the weekends Recreation was much more busy even during those three quieter hours in the midst of the night.

The defense team was going to operate seven days a week, twelve hours a day indefinitely until the problem had been resolved. Ray Raskal was very specific as he explained the situation to them. Bexley looked glum as she listened, Reuben on the other hand accepted and welcomed the news excitedly as he nodded and smiled at Ray Raskal. Cora seemed to be totally indifferent and her face was expressionless as she listened. Ray Raskal displayed no concern about the various responses by the team members he'd selected and continued to brief them further about what work areas they would be focusing upon as they listened.

Since her trip to Prohuman Inc. headquarters after she'd encountered the error messages, Martine had started to utilize the system more and more. Recreation had almost became like a drug to her as she found herself putting on her headset at every given opportunity. Jonas had now become a somewhat distant part of her life as she sought out other males to interact with. Deep down she still retained the hope however that one day she would somehow actually be able to meet Ray Raskal again.

Martine wondered at times if Ray Raskal was possibly watching her interact with other men within Recreation. Would he be that interested in one of his clients, she pondered and if so how would he interpret her interactions with some of the men she was starting to meet. One man in particular had slightly caught her attention called Damari. They'd met in the Socialite lounge and he taken her on a trip to the Recreation Theme Park.

Martine had utilized the opportunity to facilitate all the rides Penny had been too scared to enter inside with her, on their prior visit. Penny had just blankly refused to enter into the more riskier rides that rose high into the sky and plunged into the depths of the ground.

"I know they're not real or really dangerous but I'm just a little bit afraid. I'm not one for heights, they make me feel a bit dizzy." Penny had explained to Martine who'd totally understood her fears and accepted them.

Damari however had no such fears and he'd whisked Martine onto all of the rides, she'd yearned to experience since her first visit to the Theme Park. Once they'd finished enjoying their evening visit to the Recreation Theme Park, they'd walked back towards the gates, exited and arrived a few seconds later in his capsule once more. He'd stolen a kiss from her before they'd departed and Martine started to consider whether she should go further with him on their next meeting. They'd departed that evening and agreed to meet again a few days later. Damari had made his way back to the lounge as she followed him. A few minutes later he'd switched of his headset and disappeared. Martine had decided to hang back for a few minutes longer as she sat in the lounge for a moment and hoped that perhaps she would see Penny or Mavis.

Ray Raskal at that moment in time was in his office, he'd left the defense team by now as it was late in the evening and returned to his private space. He absolutely never interacted with any of the staff personally and he'd decided whilst this crisis was continuing he would not leave Prohuman Inc. headquarters and return to his home. Situated behind a wall in his office was a bedroom and bathroom both of which were hidden. The bedroom was not huge but it had a shower room attached which allowed him privacy and a place to rest if he needed it. There were large screens situated on most of the walls which he could utilize to view any part of Recreation or any part of the building any time he chose too.

Since the influx of the error messages and virus attacks, he hadn't left the building once and he'd stayed in his office quarter bedroom every night. The wardrobe had a large collection of shirts and trousers inside it. He knew deep down that it might be a week or two before he actually ventured out of the building again and he was grateful for the wardrobe provisions he'd organized at an earlier point in time.

The first day and the formation of the defense team had been tiring as Ray Raskal retired to his bedroom in his quarters and lay down on the bed he felt shattered as fatigue gushed all over his body, weighed it down and tied it firmly to the bed. He turned on Recreation and the inside of the system appeared on the large screens all around him as he started to browse visiting the many lounges, capsules and activity spaces as a spectator. After a few minutes he decide to check on Martine quickly to see what she was doing. He targeted her capsule and entered inside using the viewer control he'd created. Ray Raskal never wore a headset, he never actually had to as he didn't usually enter into Recreation himself instead he would just observe the system as an external observer from outside it. He usually just meandered through the various spaces within it in a voyeuristic manner observing whatever he felt inclined to at that particular moment in time.

Ray Raskal contemplated further as he lay in bed and watched Martine quietly, he'd now found her seated in the Socialite lounge. He knew he wanted some sexual stimulation and Martine's appearance aroused him further. He had six options available to him and he knew he'd be unable to sleep that night unless he satisfied his desire in some capacity.

The first option was the easiest and he knew it, he could access a female and a male program then program them to engage in various sexual acts with each other, the second option was the possibility of simulating an image of Martine which he could then control, making her do whatever he wanted her to, the fourth was that he could probe her headset at home and watch her through it which was a little risky and might possibly yield very little in terms of results he decided. The fifth option he contemplated would be much easier, he could just search the system and find a couple engaging in sexual activities and watch them for the arousal he required. The sixth and final option was slightly more risky but deep down Ray Raskal knew it would definitely be the most stimulating and fulfilling. He felt an urge pull him that he couldn't control, as it drew him within to participate in the sixth option. It was stronger than his usual disciplined self and as it overwhelmed him, he succumbed in defeat.

The sixth option offered him the most satisfaction, he'd actually be entering into Recreation himself, met Martine in person and participate in activities with her person. It would give him the ultimate satisfaction to the desires he craved. He couldn't sleep as the tension inside him continued to build and he felt his body surge with desires that needed relief. He made a final decision to enter inside Recreation in person and participate in a sexual encounter with Martine as he realized he could no longer resist.

Ray Raskal knew this interaction would also provide him with some visual scenes which could help ease his yearnings at a later date also so the payoff would bear fruit for him on more than one occasion. He knew it was a huge risk to actually be physical inside or outside of Recreation with any woman amongst his staff or clients groups perhaps even more so now that Prohuman was under attack. Yet the urge for satisfaction gripped and almost choked him, it was so strong and Martine so available, that he simply couldn't resist. As he lay he continued to watch her on the screen on the ceiling above his bed as he put on a headset and entered into Recreation.

The rareness of this event bore down on him as Ray Raskal acknowledged the fact that he absolutely never wore headsets, never entered the system and never participated in live sexual interactions with clients. He looked at Martine for moment as he observed her curiously and wondered how his attraction to her could prompt him to take such action.

Martine was caught off guard and totally surprised when she noticed Ray Raskal enter inside the lounge a few seconds later. He motioned towards her as he put his finger on his lips and she nodded. He led her towards a space at the end of the lounge which appeared to have no capsules running along it. He pressed a small pad on the wall nearby and a door suddenly opened. Ray Raskal led Martine inside a large apartment like room. It had a lounge inside it, a kitchen at one end and another room leading off it.

"Why are we here?" Martine asked curiously.

Ray Raskal didn't answer but instead pulled Martine closer to him and pressed her up against a wall as he closed the door behind them. He kissed her passionately and Martine reciprocated surprised and almost overwhelmed by his embrace. He tore away the leather like top and skirt she was wearing and pushed himself into her. She moaned with pleasure as he penetrated her, stimulated her, caressed her chest and touched her vigorously and frantically.

Martine surrendered to his body and gave herself to him fully unable to resist. She'd yearned for this moment, yearned for him to be inside her and yearned for him to fulfill her desires.

The night never seemed to end as they continued to sexually and orally pleasure each other and made love in every room and possible space within the apartment they were situated in. Their desire for each other felt as if it was infinite and their sexual hunger felt as if it would never be satisfied.

Eventually hours later they both collapsed onto the bed in the bedroom tired, satisfied and relieved. Martine lay in Ray Raskal's arms as she rested her head on his chest. She gazed into his eyes for a moment as she contemplated what this unplanned, unexpected interaction meant.

"Will I see you again? I mean see you again like this?" Martine asked curiously a little worried that the answer would be negative.

Ray Raskal smiled at her as he looked into her soft, green eyes. In another lifetime perhaps he would have had a real relationship with her. In another lifetime perhaps they might have even married and had children. Ray Raskal knew deep down that was what most women yearned for but he also knew due to his lifestyle and the nature of his work, it was a desire that for Martine he could never fulfill.

She would have to have those needs met somewhere else, that much he was aware off. He contemplated the possibilities, he could continue to see her within Recreation as and when he wanted too, or he could perhaps risk a purely sexual relationship in real life or he could just end it here and now as quickly as it had begun.

The real life option he knew was never going to happen. She was a client and he'd already stretched his own personal rules and boundaries by meeting her within Recreation. Pursuing real sexual or romantic liaisons with Martine in a real life environment was just asking for trouble.

"I can't answer that right now." Ray Raskal remarked as he masked the situation and his thoughts and he provided her with a kind of reassuring delay.

Ray Raskal knew that he had simple needs which he'd fulfilled for a long time through Recreation, bringing a real life Martine into his life would simply make things a lot more complex and he couldn't possibly maintain a real relationship with her. He knew he couldn't give any woman the time, attention and stability they required, not a real woman anyway, not right now and perhaps not ever.

Martine immediately understood his response, he wasn't committing himself too her and he wasn't making her any promises that he would never fulfill. He was being very casual. She surrendered to the fact that she would only perhaps have this moment to enjoy with him and that the night of passion may be all there ever was between them and though she yearned for more, she comforted herself with the moment they'd shared as she drifted off to sleep in his arms.

The next morning Martine's alarm sounded as she aroused from sleep. She found herself curled up in her comfortable chair in her alcove, still fully dressed from the night before. The headset which had slipped off her head was lying beside her actually still switched on and she put it back on her head for a second. She found herself once more back in the Socialite lounge where she'd left Damari, she searched the room curiously with her eyes, Ray Raskal was nowhere to be seen. She gazed around for her a moment somewhat confused as she walked down towards the end of the Socialite lounge where the door she'd entered the previous night with Ray Raskal had been situated. She could see the small pad on the wall but there were pads all over the walls of the lounge beside each capsule. Its presence confirmed nothing to her and as the pad was situated close to the last capsule on the wall and she knew it could easily be related to that capsule and it confirmed nothing.

Had Ray Raskal actually been there at all or had the whole situation been a dream she asked herself internally as she sighed, a little unsure. Possibly she'd fallen asleep she speculated and it had been a realization of what she wanted to happen, a desire she yearned to fulfill in real life perhaps somehow engineered by her thoughts as she'd drifted into the realms of deep slumber. She was unsure and uncertain. There was no way to verify it was actually real or that it actually happened at all. There was no real contact, no real touch, no real interaction. Whether the fantasy had simply been a manifestation of her deep internal desires or had actually occurred Martine began to resign herself to the possibility, that she may never actually know the truth.

Martine switched off the headset a few minutes later and the lounge disappeared as she remembered abruptly that she had to go to work that morning. She found herself alone once more in the lounge of her home as she glanced at the time on the clock on the wall nearby. She jumped up suddenly as she realized how quickly the time had passed, worried that she might be late for work and made her way to the bathroom to take a shower.

The defense team met the next day and Ray Raskal gave all the staff within the team the morning briefing. Haiden, Cora and Brice, he trusted implicitly to resolve the problem quickly and competently. Bexley and Reuben were there more or less to provide support to his top developer, advanced systems engineer and security specialist. Ray Raskal knew that he could involve more staff but he'd satisfied himself that these five would be sufficient for now. If Cora, Haiden and Brice couldn't resolve the problem, it was unlikely that anyone else within the company would be able to, that much Ray Raskal knew.

Brice was his most advanced systems engineer and he hardly spoke to anyone at work but when he did so he was extremely polite. He had light brown skin and a slight Mediterranean accent.

Ray Raskal sat at a desk in the small meeting room, he'd allocated to the defense team as he listened to Cora, Brice and Haiden who were discussing and deliberating the facts regarding the situation. Bexley and Reuben listened attentively as they observed the three specialists formulating models and running simulations in the back end of Recreation whilst they attempted to find the source of the Virus.

Ray Raskal's mind drifted back for a moment to the prior nights' escapades with Martine as he listened. He'd needed some relief, he'd needed something and he'd known from her visit to Prohuman HQ she was his for the taking. Martine had fully succumbed to him and his desires. She hadn't played coy or hard to get and had simply yielded to him and given him what he needed, what they both needed at that precise moment in time. He knew deep down however it was something he couldn't risk doing ever again. He'd taken a huge risk intercepting and interacting with her; it was not a situation he could dare to repeat. There would be repercussions if he did and he knew it. She'd want more, he'd yearn for more and it would create a conflict that right now he couldn't afford the time to deal with.

Haiden suddenly interrupted his thoughts.

"I've found a possible solution." Haiden remarked. "We're not sure of the cause or source yet but we can block it for it now. We have to shut down one of the activity menus for a few days and block the virus by rewriting some parts of the underlying programming in that area of Recreation." He explained.

Ray Raskal nodded.

"Do whatever it takes to stop it." He replied. "A few days lack of functionality is better than the virus spreading and corrupting the whole system."

Haiden nodded.

"Will we ever know the source?" Ray Raskal asked as he stood up and prepared to leave the room.

Haiden, Cora and Brice looked at him and Ray Raskal could tell by their faces they were unsure. He had no desire to distract them at the moment with alternative investigations and enquiries, the functionality and continuation of the system was the ultimate priority right now and he knew it therefore he simply pushed the question to the back of his mind, shook his head and departed without waiting for a response. They understood by his actions that the question he'd posed to them did not require an answer at that precise moment in time which relieved them as none of them had one.

Ray Raskal left the team to continue with the system repairs, satisfied that the situation was now partially under control and that everything would be resolved within a few days. The crisis had been contained and controlled. Ray Raskal was satisfied, he could finally relax.

Martine continued for a few more weeks to live in expectation and hopefulness as she utilized Recreation at every available opportunity, wishing for another interlude with Ray Raskal. Her efforts were futile however, Ray Raskal never appeared or met her within Recreation and as time passed by she eventually began to accept her hopes and expectations may never be met.

Martine knew deep inside, she couldn't even raise the matter as an issue with Ray Raskal directly as she was still a little unsure that it actually ever really happened at all. She started to engage in interactions with other men once more and engage their advances, though deep in heart she held the buried feelings of what could have been if Ray Raskal had returned.

The question of whether Ray Raskal would ever return now lay somewhere in Martine's mind dormant, buried under the two large rocks of maybe and possibly. Martine forced herself to move on as she decided that the issue of Ray Raskal's return was uncertain but the reality that she had one life to live was very certain and each precious day she waited, she was perhaps waiting in vain. She succumbed to defeat as she realized that waiting for Ray Raskal to return didn't increase the chances or likelihood that he ever would.

MIRRORS DON'T LIE

A few months had passed since Martine's initial sign up for Prohuman's services and she had continued to enjoy everything about Recreation. One morning however as she woke up and prepared for work, she made her way to the bathroom still partially asleep; she gazed up at the mirror in front of her as she brushed her hair and a few seconds later as she looked at the brush in her hand, she felt a gush of horror rush through her body. She shook with fear as she gazed at the mass of hair that had accumulated on the brush, she picked at the strands confused and distraught for a moment.

Martine gazed back up at the mirror rapidly and was horrified as she noticed a bald spot in the middle of her head. Tears started to fill her eyes as she began to cough. A few minutes later her mouth filled with liquid and she felt the urge to spit, she emptied the contents of her mouth into the bathroom sink briskly. She gasped in shock as she noticed the bright, red blood which now lay spotted and collated in a small pool in the white sink in front of her. Its scarlet hue spotted all over the ceramic white alarmed her. Her arm began to itch below her silk pajama top, she rushed as she pulled her sleeve up higher and scratched her arm to appease it.

Underneath her sleeve the bare skin now exposed a black and blue rash that was clearly forming. Martine shook her head with disbelief, looked into the mirror once more and held her arm up towards it to see the extent of the bruise type rash more clearly. There was no denying its existence as she started to tremble with fear and wondered what could have possibly caused it.

Martine made her way back to the lounge and sat down for a moment as she contemplated what she should do next. She had absolutely no idea what was going on. She hadn't changed skin products, bath foams, shower creams or soap powder recently. Her health and body had been in prime condition for a while and she hadn't suffered from even the slightest cold or flu. She'd attended the doctor's clinic a few months ago for a general health checkup and she'd been perfectly fine.

The phone lay on the table nearby and she glanced at it thoughtfully for a few moments as she contemplated who she should call. The only real change in her life recently had been her participation in Recreation. She thought about further and decided it wouldn't be a good idea to call Prohuman Inc. in case these issues were related to her participation within the system. Finally she decided the best person to call would be Jonas; she'd try to establish if he was experiencing any similar symptoms and that would help her identify if indeed this deterioration in health was related to her participation in Recreation or not. Martine paused for a moment before she picked up the phone to look for his number. She hadn't spoken to Jonas for a while which made her feel a little unsure for a moment about whether or not she should actually call him. Finally she succumbed to her curiosity and desire for answers and decided to do so as she touched the screen of her phone to initiate the call. The phone rang for a few moments before he answered it, he sounded sleepy and as if he'd just woken up as she listened to him greet her.

"Jonas can we meet please?" Martine urged.

The phone went silent and although his silence only lasted for a few seconds it felt like much longer to Martine as she waited for him to respond.

"Sure, when?" He finally replied.

"Can we meet later today?" Martine asked rapidly relieved that he was agreeing to meet her.

Their friendship had been totally neglected for some time and she'd been slightly unsure as she'd made the call that he would even be willing to make time for her anymore and agree to a meeting. She quickly pushed him for a commitment as she emphasized the importance and urgency in her request. Jonas agreed after a few more minutes as they confirmed a time and location that was a mid-point and convenient for them both. Martine ended the call and started to prepare for the day ahead.

The itching on Martine's arm from the rash still bothered her throughout the day but she tried to ignore it and avoid scratching it further. Before she'd left home to meet Jonas that day, she'd searched the bathroom cabinet for a soothing cold cream to smear over it and that was relieving the itching somewhat.

Later that day as Martine arrived at the agreed coffee shop and entered inside, she discovered

Jonas was already there waiting for her. He ordered a coffee for her as she sat down opposite him. Martine noticed almost immediately as she sat that his hair was looking slightly greyer than it had the last time she'd seen him.

"Jonas, there's something wrong." She started to explain. "There's strange blueish, black rashes and lumps appearing on my skin, my hair is falling out and I'm coughing up blood."

Martine lifted her sleeve up and exposed the rash on her arm to illustrate to Jonas exactly what she meant as she spoke.

"I know it's happening to me too." He replied reassuringly as he nodded in agreement. "And I'm aging."

"Is it only happening to us?" Martine enquired as she looked at him curiously.

Confusion laced and filled her bright green eyes and Jonas emphasized with her immediately. Jonas shook his head and shrugged in response.

"I'm not totally sure, but I'll do a bit of research and try to find out. I'll speak to a few more people at Recreation and see if anyone else is suffering the same symptoms." Jonas replied as he attempted to reassure her, he touched her arm gently as he spoke. "Don't worry, we'll get to the bottom of this."

Martine began to nod appreciatively, partially relieved to discover that she was not alone in her suffering. The coffee Jonas had ordered for her arrived and she spooned in some sugar as they continued their discussion.

"What should we do in the meantime?" She asked. "Should I see a doctor?"

Jonas paused for a second unsure before he responded. It was probably a good idea he thought for someone to consult a doctor and he knew he was overloaded at work right now and had very little free time in which to do so. He'd also just agreed to start researching the situation which meant he'd definitely have less free time to indulge in any such appointments.

"Yes sure you do that and I'll call you when I have more leads about what's going on. Don't use your headset again in the meantime just in case." He insisted. "You could make it worse."

Martine nodded in agreement. She had absolutely no intention of doing so for now, she'd been totally put off the entire idea of participating in Prohuman until she could be sure what was causing the symptoms she was experiencing.

For the next few days she attended work as usual. She wore a bandana over her head to cover her hair loss and to avoid any awkward questions being asked. After a few days however one of her work colleagues began to notice her strange headwear, a mature woman Trudy who worked in the finance department found an opportunity to corner her and ask her about it, determined to find out what was going on.

"Why are you wearing that on your head?" She asked curiously in a hushed tone as they stood in a corner of the staff kitchen. "I've noticed you wearing it for a few days now. Did you dye your hair the wrong color or something?"

Martine looked at her for a moment unsure whether she should explain the truth to her or not. How could she possibly reveal to this mature, sensible woman that she was indulging in a fantasy, leisure activity that was somewhat surreal and that it was causing some kind of negative impact to her health. The whole topic was difficult to explain and Martine knew it. Trudy would probably think it was strange and weird.

"I'm having a medical problem and it's affected my hair and scalp." Martine finally blurted out after a few minutes pause.

Trudy nodded in understanding as she listened, she assumed immediately that she knew what was really going on.

"Chemotherapy does that dear." She reassured Martine as she touched her hand gently and attempted to comfort her as she drew closer. "Don't worry I won't say a word to anyone." She whispered as Martine nodded in response.

Trudy walked over towards the hot water dispenser nearby and Martine wondered for a moment if she should correct her incorrect assumption. After a few moments she decided not to and determined it was best to allow Trudy's curiosity to be satisfied by her own response. Correcting her now would just prompt more awkward questions which she had no desire to answer, not yet anyway.

"How was your weekend Trudy?" She asked quickly anxious to divert the topic of conversation to something lighter as she followed her over to the dispenser and started to prepare her own mug of coffee.

Trudy smiled as she welcomed the opportunity to discuss her personal life. Her mouth started to gush with details of her weekend as Martine smiled and started to fill up her cup. It was almost as if her mouth was releasing a stream of water which seemed to flow more quickly than the water flowed out of the water dispenser Martine mused internally. She listened quietly and nodded her head gently.

"It was amazing fun, my husband and I took the children to the theatre. They absolutely loved it." She replied nodding enthusiastically. "Do you ever go?"

Martine shook her head as she reflected internally about her situation whilst she continued to partially listen to Trudy. Part of her mind was focused on her conversation and the other part of delved back and forth into her own thoughts. Trudy carried on revealing the intimate details of her weekend as Martine contemplated how different their lives were. Trudy would never understand Recreation; the artificial, alternative reality that fully occupied her leisure time, one that Martine had paid a huge sum of money to participate in. Trudy would probably think she was too lonely and bored and start trying to set her up on blind dates she thought silently.

Martine continued to smile and nod at regular intervals as Trudy spoke, to reassure her that she was listening and giving her, her full attention. After a few more minutes, Trudy glanced at her watch and realized she needed to leave to attend a meeting. Martine smiled and nodded in understanding as she excused herself, rushed off and left Martine in the kitchen alone. Once alone she sighed with relief, glad that she had escaped further interrogation and the stress of any other awkward questions Trudy may have continued to pose to her.

The rest of the week was relatively quiet as Martine simply attended work and went straight home. There were no social or leisure activities at all and she avoided utilizing the headset as she'd agreed with Jonas. On the Friday evening Jonas finally called her and urged her to come round to his house.

"I have a friend here." Jonas explained. "He's a professional hacker." He remarked. "We're going to hack the Prohuman system and see what we can find."

"I'll be right over." Martine replied as she smiled satisfied that Jonas was indeed handling the situation and that his promises had not just been empty words.

She ended the call quickly and a few minutes later prepared to leave. She was now feeling slightly excited at the prospect of being involved with a hacker and them all colluding together to spy on Prohuman. It was all very risqué and it satisfied her to know that finally they'd be taking action to uncover the truth.

When she arrived at Jonas's apartment, Jonas and his acquaintance had already started the Prohuman Inc. system interrogation. Jonas showed her in and she entered the lounge eagerly.

"Did you manage to find anything out yet or get inside the system?" She asked enthusiastically as she sat down one of the chairs opposite a young man.

He glanced up at her briefly for a second as she entered and smiled. Martine's arrival interrupted his concentration which had been focused on the screen situated in the table in front of him.

"This is Lamar." Jonas explained to Martine as he sat down next to Lamar on the sofa and gazed at the screen Lamar had been fixated on.

Jonas looked back up at Martine's face for a moment and noticed that although she was smiling he could sense underlying strain. Martine he thought wasn't the same person he'd initially met at the Prohuman Inc. headquarters on the day of their induction and he could tell. Something had changed, something was definitely different, aside from the physical changes, he could sense her spirit was now somehow broken and damaged. Her lust and excitement for life, somehow impaired as if the lifeblood had been sapped out of her and her lifespan drained. If life was like a pool of water Martine's core had been sucked dry and was lying like a dehydrated leaf on the floor next to her, crinkled, shriveled and trailing behind her on the floor wherever she went. She wasn't the same person, but Jonas also knew neither was he.

"Lamar is a professional hacker." Jonas explained. "We attended some professional courses together several years ago." Jonas continued as he introduced Lamar properly to her.

Martine gazed at one of the screens on the table in front of them and smiled. There were about five screens in front of them all various shapes and sizes, some were connected to each other and others sat functioning independently. She stared for a moment in awe of all the equipment they were utilizing to perform their task.

"What did you guys find out?" Martine urged anxiously, hungry for more details regarding their discoveries.

"A lot." Jonas verified. "We found out the founder of Prohuman had a similar company a few years before under a different company name. They were closed down due to hazardous uses of technology that were detrimental to people's health." He explained.

"How was he allowed to start Prohuman Inc.? I mean didn't they blacklist him after that happened." Martine asked curiously a little taken back that the man she had been so physically attracted too and even perhaps had a surreal night of passion with could potentially be a monster.

"You'd expect that right?" Jonas continued. "Apparently he escaped liability as he wasn't a main director of the company. He had an employment contract and was purely hired as an executive of some sort. He managed to secure some investors who were the legal directors and the face of the company. They took the blame ultimately for his experimentation."

Martine nodded in understanding as she started to understand the fullness of the information she was being presented with. Not only was Ray Raskal responsible for the horror they were experiencing, he'd done it before and got away with it.

Lamar interjected with his own analysis at this point.

"People died as a result of using some of the technology the Prohuman Inc. framework is built on. There is some kind of radioactive material that was used in the headsets that's dangerous to the human biological structure." Lamar explained. "It supposedly enhances the user experience and makes it more lucid and real. Ray Raskal tried to create an equilibrium using chemical components and developed a compound, to try and negate its effects. However as you can see his attempts to neutralize the impact on the human body were unsuccessful or failed in some instances. We can't be sure just yet off the full impact of this failure."

Martine nodded as she listened, though the topic of chemical components and radioactive materials was a little out of her depth. She'd never paid much attention in chemistry classes at high school, she'd found the topics it encapsulated very dull; she'd quickly disposed of it as part of her study program at the earliest opportunity possible.

"Do you think it's affected anyone else who uses Recreation?" She asked as she began to be distracted and concerned regarding the welfare of Mavis and Penny.

"Definitely." Lamar replied.

"What can we do now?" Martine asked them both alarmed and confused.

"We can try and contact everyone and expose the situation. The more people there are standing against Ray Raskal the better." Jonas replied.

Martine started to feel torn internally as her stomach began to knot and the weight sank to the bottom of her gut with a thump. At last she'd found this deliciously, profoundly handsome, intelligent, assertive man only to discover in reality he was a monster. Her internal attraction for Ray Raskal was hidden and Jonas had never been aware of it, therefore he had no idea how she felt and the emotional turmoil these disturbing revelations were causing inside her.

The choice that she knew she had to make was severe but there was no real choice and deep within her she realized that. Whatever she had once felt for Ray Raskal, she knew she now had to chastise, whatever emotional connection she'd developed to him she now had to totally crucify.

She smiled as she mused internally, if Ray Raskal saw her looking like this he probably wouldn't even give her a second glance again anyway. Ray Raskal had never returned to her within Recreation and she could never fully be sure they'd ever spent the night together in there anyway. Martine's severing of the emotional bond and feelings she had for him within her would probably not be something that even mattered much to Ray Raskal anyway she concluded. The thought that his recklessness and negligence had inflicted physical damage to her body horrified her and the attraction she'd once felt had started to evaporate as fascination and admiration suddenly spiraled downwards and started to transform into hatred and disgust.

Martine knew she was not that special to Ray Raskal that he would face up to his actions for her. There were a million women out there that Ray Raskal had easy access to and she was under absolutely no illusions, he would be able to replace her in his life in two seconds very easily indeed if he wanted to and perhaps she thought, he may have already done so. Ray Raskal had avoided the consequences of his mistakes and experiments once and deep within her Martine knew if he was confronted about them now, he'd simply deny any accusations and avoid them again in any way he could.

She considered for a moment that he'd probably also met other women just like her in the past, other clients whom he'd serviced, some of whom may have even died. He hadn't changed for them, why would he change for her, she asked herself these probing questions and confronted the reality but she knew the answers already. He wouldn't change for anyone, he hadn't changed last time and he wouldn't change this time.

Martine started to acknowledge the harsh truths regarding the reality of Ray Raskal as the facts sank in. Her body became weary and heavy as she absorbed the truth.

"Have you been to see the doctor yet?" Jonas asked as he remembered their last conversation at the coffee shop.

Martine shook her head. "Not yet. I was putting it off really until you had a bit more information." She explained.

Jonas appreciated her desire for more clarity before she took action; he could sense Martine was terrified by the whole situation and predicament they now faced. Deep down he knew he was too. There was some information, they'd uncovered, that he hadn't yet divulged to Martine; he feared doing so as he knew it would make her even more alarmed and distressed. Every director that had run Ray Raskal's last venture alongside him was now dead.

"Will we ever be able to reverse the effects on our health of the headsets?" Martine asked softly as she looked into his eyes, fearing the answer she might receive. "Do you think Penny is ok?"

Jonas looked at her and hesitated for a moment before replying. He had no direct answers for her right now and he knew it, it was an area he hadn't managed to research yet and he hadn't checked on Penny at all or her wellbeing. He'd been too preoccupied attempting to discover the root cause of their inflictions, he'd spent very little time focusing on finding any potential remedies.

"I mean look at us Jonas we're aging and we don't know how long it will continue or how much worse it will become." Martine replied as she stood up and looked at herself in the large mirror that hung on a nearby wall inside Jonas's lounge.

Jonas stood up and glanced in the mirror also as he stood slightly behind her and looked at their aging appearance.

"Mirrors don't lie Jonas. Whatever false life we experienced in that system, we can now see the real manifestation of reality here in our lives and bodies within the mirror." Martine murmured sadly.

Jonas nodded, he knew she was right. He'd accessed Recreation once more since he'd noticed the aging and deterioration of his health. Inside Recreation his physical appearance within the lounges and activity rooms was exactly the same as it had been the first day he'd attended his induction sessions and his personal profile on the system appeared totally unchanged.

Jonas had stopped seeing Alivia though he'd met her quite a few times and even indulged and participated in a few sexual liaisons, their romantic interludes had only spanned a couple of months after their initial meeting and now had ceased totally. The sexual intimacy between them had never managed to quite reach the potential Jonas had hoped it would and he'd never been actually able to realize that first exhilarating experience and the moments of passion he'd enjoyed with her inside Recreation that first day, in reality.

Once his hair had started greying and the rash developed on his skin, Jonas started to make excuses as he attempted to avoid her requests to him once again in real life. He'd attempted to maintain some contact with her within Recreation but after he cancelled a few of their appointments in real life, Alivia started to avoid him even there. Now he no longer saw here anywhere as the phone calls dried up and Alivia he assumed, moved on.

For a moment he cast his mind further to the topic of Alivia as he curiously wondered if she had also been affected as they had. His mind soon wandered back towards the issue Martine had raised of finding a potential solution. The possibility of never being able to return to the life they'd once had now started to scare him, he had no answers for Martine or himself.

"I'm not sure Martine." He finally replied, his voice sounded defeated and dejected as he felt waves of inner despair wash over his body.

He yearned to reassure her that everything would be fine, they would be fine, they'd return to how they once were physically and continue to live full productive lives but deep down he knew, they both had to face the grim reality, there were no such reassurances or comforting words he could provide right now and Jonas couldn't bare to lie to her. Providing Martine with false hope that everything would be fine when he wasn't certain it would be, was the cowardly way out and he knew it.

Martine left soon after and he stood by the lounge window as he watched her leave, his body felt heavy, almost tied to the ground with weights on his feet of sorrow and despair. Jonas began to speculate further the thought that there may be no actual cure and wondered how they would both live knowing that they were going to die prematurely in the tangled web of death Ray Raskal had created.

Martine entered inside her car as he watched, drove down the road and disappeared into the distance. Jonas shook his head then went to sit back down once more beside Lamar as they continued to interrogate the system. Lamar was the best hacker Jonas knew and there was an element of certainty within him that by the time he was finished with Ray Raskal's files there would be nothing they didn't know about him, his past and his experiments.

Jonas touched a screen nearby as he attempted to search for answers to the question Martine had posed. He had no certainty that his search would yield results and as he started to search for a possible reversal, a solution or some ounce of hope the damage to their bodies could somehow be repaired, he felt slightly demotivated.

Two days later Athena received an urgent request to attend Ray Raskal's office for a meeting. He'd emailed her and Athena instantly felt reassured and comforted once more by his message. Ray Raskal had requested her presence and assistance in an emergency situation. It encouraged her as she immediately cheered up and prepared to attend. Athena was still the one he turned too and leaned on in moments of need and his message proved this. Athena entered inside his office a few minutes later and smiled enthusiastically as he nodded his head towards her.

"Sit down please Athena." He urged.

Athena participated eagerly but as she did so she observed as she gazed at his face, it was filled with tension. Now the once handsome, vibrant face of Ray Raskal drooped somehow and appeared to look almost like a willow tree whose branches swept the ground as if burdened with the universe's despairs.

"How can I help?" Athena asked enthusiastically in an attempt to lift his spirits.

Ray Raskal glanced up at her as he rubbed his head with his hands. He stood up and started to pace the room.

"We've had an intruder Athena." He explained. "They've hacked into our system."

"Why would someone do that?" Athena asked curiously, very confused by his news.

Ray Raskal looked at her for a moment as he pondered as too how much he actually trusted her. The events of the past and his last company directorship flooded through his mind, he couldn't explain that away by simply glossing over the issues, real people had died and those were real facts. Athena would never understand and there was a possibility she would betray him if she knew the truth, he pondered over how he should respond to her question as he continued to pace the room.

Ray Raskal was also very much aware of the impact he had on women, they adored him and within him, he knew Athena was no different. He could sense her emotional and physical attraction to him, though he'd never been physical with her or encouraged such intimacy. He knew however Athena would yield to any such advances from him if he decided to approach her.

Her willingness to work overtime late into the evenings whenever he asked, coupled with her happiness when he was attentive towards her and her dismay when he wasn't, indicated she was definitely attracted to him. He also knew right now that her attraction to him was a strength he may need to draw on and manipulate at some point in the future to guarantee her complete loyalty to him, Prohuman Inc. and Recreation.

The decision loomed in his mind but a few seconds later he arrived at the destination of conclusion, Ray Raskal decided to save the card of attraction for further down the line. The situation was not yet that critical he thought that such desperate measures had to be engaged in just yet. Ray Raskal was fully aware also that

Athena was a smart woman, if he suddenly jumped into bed with her right now in the midst of a crisis situation, she'd be suspicious. If he was going to enter into any kind of false romantic relationship that allowed him to draw upon Athena's support, he knew he'd have to work up to it a little more gradually. His attraction and interest in her had to appear to Athena to be very natural and not contrived.

For now Ray Raskal decided that he would leave that rock resting in the ground, he concluded that for the moment he wasn't actually sure there was such a huge problem just yet. The last thing he wanted to do was arouse Athena's urges without a necessary reason to do so.

Ray Raskal prided himself on his success which he knew lay predominantly in the very fact he did not have a time consuming relationship to maintain with a woman on his hands. He was not answerable to any woman and there were no distractions. Athena was a strong woman and he knew once he unleashed her passions, he wouldn't be able to just switch them off again. She'd never accept that, she'd seek a deeper commitment from him; one she felt she deserved and was entitled too and for now he wasn't in a rush to make such a commit to anyone, not even a pretentious one.

His sexual urges were for now being fulfilled and met fully voyeuristically as he watched stimulations and people interact inside Recreation. Sometimes he observed couples having sex and utilized it as a source of arousal. None of the engineers could track his access to the system he'd designed and created which meant his movements within it were totally untraceable. That anonymity provided him with a liberty within Recreation that no one else possessed which meant for now, he had absolutely no need to pursue a sexual relationship with her. His emotional needs were minimal and to Ray Raskal the only potential advantage of indulging in a romantic relationship with a woman would be to utilize and lean on her as a support base.

The situation though difficult was still manageable he decided and he had no urgent desire to rush. He weighed up the time and attention such a commitment would require from him and his own requirements. If the issue escalated further he decided Athena's support may be required and he may have to trust her but for now, he was reluctant to commit himself further to her.

"I'm not sure Athena." He finally replied quietly as he decided not to divulge too much information to Athena just yet. "Perhaps they were trying to steal trade secrets."

He looked at her face for a moment to observe her reaction as he suddenly realized how unconvincing his response had been. His voice had wavered as it betrayed his lie and he wondered for a moment if Athena had noticed. Athena he knew spent a lot of time with him, more than anyone else at Prohuman and if anyone could sense he was lying he thought, it would definitely be her.

"When your successful you become everyone's target. They all want the life you have without making the sacrifices required to attain it." He continued as he attempted to reinforce the lie he'd already told her as if somehow that would make it more convincing.

Athena nodded as if she understood and he was instantly put at ease. Ray Raskal knew he couldn't read her mind but trusted her feelings and attraction to him to suppress any doubts she may have in him. He knew emotional attachment and attraction were the two biggest weaknesses of the female gender. Once a woman loved a man her sight quite often would be blinded by her emotions to his flaws, imperfections and sometimes even to his sins. Ray Raskal knew at some point in the future, he may need to align with her and engage her strength and that she would be blinded by her emotional attachment to him. He may have to rely on that weakness to protect him he thought as he gazed at Athena's face quietly for a moment.

Athena had the potential to be a strong ally and Ray Raskal knew this. Her support would be immensely helpful to him if the situation became more difficult for him and he knew that one day soon he may need Athena's protection. If Ray Raskal allowed Athena to love him; her feelings for him to fully manifest, develop and become totally engaged, he knew deep within she would protect him and his interests at all costs.

REALITY VS REALITY

The health of Martine and Jonas continued to deteriorate as each day passed by. They tried to as much as possible to disguise it to those around them but it was becoming harder and harder and their ailments more and more obvious. Martine sought permission to work from home and opted out of attending the office on work days. She knew that eventually she would have to admit the truth to someone and was trying to avoid doing so for as long as she possibly could. Luckily for Martine, unlike a traditional office working environment, she worked almost like a freelancer, mainly attending clients homes to plan interior design work, which meant the majority of her working hours she wasn't based at the head office. However, she usually attended two or three days a week, just to check in and update client records. Her line manager, Sadia, granted her permission to perform these tasks from home for a while though she was slightly concerned about Martine's request.

"Is everything fine Martine?" She'd queried when Martine approached her to ask for permission.

"Yes I'm fine really." Martine had reassured her.

"It's just, well, you're wearing a head scarf a lot and now you're asking to work from home. Is there anything I should know? Are you suffering any kind of health problems?" Sadia had enquired gently.

Martine had smiled and shaken her head.

"It's just a personal matter." She'd explained. "Nothing huge, but working from home for a while will help."

Sadia had been accommodating and nodded in agreement as she replied granting her permission. "That's fine work from home as long as you need. We value your work and we try to accommodate people's needs when we can; working from home for a while is not a huge problem. It's a reasonable request, after all you've been with us for years."

Martine had smiled with relief, she appreciated Sadia's flexibility; not every workplace or line manager would have been so understanding and she knew it. Deep inside she realized that the nature of her work had probably helped, it meant she wasn't in the office that much which meant the impact of her absence would be minimal. She felt grateful for a second that she'd chosen interior design as a career and not pursued something more restrictive.

"Ask one of the IT guys to give you a laptop, an interaction device and login so that you can access our system more easily from home." Sadia had instructed. "That way you'll have everything you need."

Martine had nodded gratefully and made her way to the IT department in adherence to her instructions. From now on though she was acutely aware that the situation would continue to spiral downwards and she had no idea just how much longer she'd even be able to keep up with her interior design workload commitments.

Luckily for Martine as she knew she was just a designer. That meant she never had to actually participate in any heavy like physically intensive tasks such as painting houses or moving furniture around. She feared what impact her deteriorating health would have had on her life if this had not been this case as she realized it would have been much more significant financially.

Now she was working from home and today her day was empty. She'd finished her last client assignment early, the day before and there was a day in-between, before her next assignment was due to start. She sat in the lounge and contemplated what to do with the rest of her day. The Prohuman Inc. headset lay on the table nearby and she was tempted to use it as she looked at it.

The temptation to be her usual, younger, healthy and more vibrant self, appealed to her as the urge pulled her internally to participate in Recreation once more. Recreation where in that false reality, her body would be perfectly fine, attractive and appealing once again. Her desire grew as it continued to entice her. She yearned for the validation she knew she was used too. Inside Recreation she was acutely aware that men would still admire her and view her as she once was; before she'd started aging, before her hair had started falling out and before the strange bruises had started to appear on her skin.

She touched the headset delicately, she knew that if she dared to put it on her head, she'd evoke the aging process once more and there would possibly be physical consequences. She stood up and looked in the mirror that hung on the wall nearby for a second and mourned the aging, decaying carcass her body had become. The reality of who she once was, was not the reality of who she was now. To exist in and enjoy the reality she knew deep within she was entitled too, she knew she'd have to embrace and enter Recreation once more.

Jonas was also facing a similar conundrum but his own unique dilemma had an additional yearning as he desired to engage in the energetic sexual liaisons he'd once enjoyed with Alivia once again. Those interactions had made him feel alive and he lusted to experience that feeling once more. The aging affects had taken their toll on his body and his physical appearance become worse and he'd had to take some time off work. Most of his on call shifts where he provided support to employees outside work hours could be done from home and he was still able to participate in those but some of his work tasks he couldn't perform. Some tasks required his attendance at Resolute the company he worked for and demanded his presence at head office.

Jonas had requested sick leave and luckily his boss had been very understanding and granted it to him as he'd never requested sick leave before. He still participated in his on call work but Jonas now found he had vast expanses of time during the day and evenings that were unoccupied. Some of these vacant hours he facilitated as he kept himself busy with further research into Prohuman Inc. and other hours he utilized to continue the search for a potential solution to reverse the aging process. He also continued fervently to look for a possible cure to the bruise like rashes he and Martine now had all over their bodies.

The enticement of possible sexual liaisons however occasionally danced through his memories, thoughts and mind as he yearned to experience sexual gratification as the healthy, vibrant, masculine male he had once been in the not so distant past. The depletion of his body meant that he no longer felt comfortable to even approach a woman right now in the real world. His confidence waned as his impairment started to cause a heaviness in his spirit. The yearning today was strong and as he sat in the lounge he desperately tried to distract himself from the urges he felt within. He poured a strong, black coffee into a cup from a nearby pot and tried to focus on the screens in front of him. Lamar had left some his equipment and Jonas started to focus on it as it lay in front of him. Lamar had been coming back and forth from his apartment quite regularly now as they attempted to discover more and more information and the equipment Lamar left in his lounge was growing each time visited and left another gadget behind. Jonas smiled for a moment as he looked around his lounge which now looked more like a computer operation room than an actual domestic lounge, he'd faced the challenge straight on and the impact of Prohuman Inc.'s technology on his life and health and that thought that comforted him slightly and made him feel proud. Deep within he knew that it would have been easier to run away, hide from it or ignore it. It had been a huge challenge and a difficult one with serious implications and he had borne it like a man.

The hunger for intimate intertwining's once more surfaced and distracted him as they dug deeper into his consciousness and state of existence. He simply couldn't focus. He picked up the phone nearby and decided to call Martine. Right now Martine and Lamar were the only people that he could spend any length of time with, without a hundred questions being asked regarding his situation and health. His family he knew if he contacted them would intrude and want to know what was going on. He'd only called his mother a few times in the past few months and at this point in time she had absolutely no idea what he was experiencing. He couldn't face the questions right now his physical presence would evoke and he knew he couldn't face her. Lamar right now he knew was busy attending to a freelance work assignment and therefore wasn't available which meant Martine right now was his only option for companionship and the only person who might provide him with a distraction from the physical urges that pulled at him from within.

"Can you come over?" He asked as she answered his call.

"Sure." Martine replied enthusiastically. "I'll make my way over now."

Jonas sighed with relief as he put down the phone and ended the call. Martine's visit would save him from the temptation's he was finding harder and harder to resist as each day passed and her presence and the distraction was something he urgently needed today.

Martine prepared to make her way to Jonas, glad that he'd interrupted her and that she now had something very real to do that would keep her away from the artificial enjoyment she was tempted to explore once more within Recreation. Her family had called her several times and she'd made several excuses not to attend family gatherings and events. It was becoming harder and harder to excuse herself however and they were starting to become a little suspicious.

"Is there anything I should know?" Her mother had asked on one occasion when she'd called, confused by her daughter's sudden unwillingness to participate in family events.

Martine had been reluctant to tell her the truth, not wishing to worry her or disturb her emotionally.

"Not at all mum." Martine had reassured her.

"You'd tell me if something was wrong?" Veronica had pressed, unsatisfied with Martine's response.

"Sure mum. I'd definitely tell you if something was wrong." Martine replied as she'd attempted to reassure her.

"Have you got a new boyfriend, you don't want us to meet?" Veronica had teased. "Is he married, is he really a she?"

Martine had laughed at her response, seeing a married man or woman; things which some mothers and families would possibly not approve off, would be a welcome problem to face right now rather than the reality of the tribulation she was actually enduring. It was becoming harder and harder to avoid them however and eventually Martine knew she would have to face them or they'd come and find her. Martine was worried about what their reaction would be when that happened, she loved her parents very deeply and had no desire to alarm them. She prayed that Jonas would find a cure before that situation presented itself and they came to find her.

Martine parked her car outside Jonas's apartment and made her way towards the outside door. Luckily she thought she was still able to drive and that to Martine was a huge blessing as it meant she wasn't stuck at home all the time or reliant on public transport, where prying eyes would stare and speculate about her appearance.

"How are you feeling today?" Jonas asked as he opened the front door of his apartment wide and she stepped inside the door.

"I'm ok." She remarked. "I'm a little worse but I've stayed away from the headset so I think the deterioration is a little more gradual now." She explained.

Jonas nodded in agreement. "Same here. We have to be strong and stay away from the headsets. They're killing us."

Martine nodded in agreement as she removed her jacket and he hung it on a nearby coat hook. They made their way into the lounge and Martine sat down on the sofa.

"Fancy a coffee?" Jonas asked.

"Sure." Martine nodded enthusiastically as Jonas walked to the kitchen nearby, she stood up and followed him. "Did you manage to find out if other people are facing the same type of problems we are?" She asked as her curiosity prompted her to ascertain more information regarding the status of other Prohuman clients.

Martine was still rather worried about Penny and Mavis and their wellbeing. Jonas looked at her for a moment then continued to pour the dark, black, rich coffee into a nearby mug. Martine smiled at the aroma emanating from the coffee beans as it began to fill her nostrils.

"Lamar found out there are about five thousand clients registered to participate in Recreation. It would be impossible to track them all down." Jonas explained. "However he did manage to find about thirty people that live within a ten mile radius and he suggested we should check on some of them."

Martine nodded in agreement as Jonas handed her the coffee cup, she spooned in some sugar and a dash of milk before they made their way back to the sofa in the lounge once more. Jonas sat beside her and started to show her a list on one of the screens nearby.

"This is the list of people that Lamar provided, I have their addresses, phone numbers and photo's. Calling them is a bad idea, it may scare them, but we could easily sit on the street outside their homes for a few hours and try to identify them that way and verify their situations." Jonas continued.

Martine nodded in agreement.

"Yes that's practical and it should be obvious if they are affected, we should be able to tell quite easily if they've aged by comparing them to their profile photos." Martine agreed. "When do we start?"

"Straight away." Jonas remarked as he picked up his car keys, laptop and phone from the table. "Once you've finished your coffee we'll go."

Martine nodded and smiled, grateful that this activity was going to provide a longer, active and more complex distraction than she'd originally envisaged a visit to Jonas's home would entail; the power of her internal desires would be numbed, neutralized and easier to overcome for a while now and that comforting thought reassured her. It was likely she knew that they would be busy for days with this task and she was relieved.

A few minutes later once her coffee was finished, she followed Jonas out into the hallway. She smiled gently for the first time in a while as she passed the mirror in the lounge on her way out and caught sight of her reflection. In the presence of Jonas she felt comfortable, she didn't mind as much how she looked right now. Jonas understood the strange rashes that were appearing on her skin as he had them too. He understood the aging, greying hair and bald patches hidden underneath the bandana and headscarves she was now accustomed to wearing. There were no awkward explanations required or uncomfortable feelings. For the first time in a while she realized she actually felt comfortable about how she looked in the presence of someone else.

Situated in his office at Prohuman Inc. Ray Raskal continued to evaluate and assess the level of damage the intrusion had caused to the system. Unlike the virus attacks which had been corporate sabotage, this attack he knew was different. The intrusion this time had been more personal; the invisible intruder and enemy had delved into and explored back end files, as they sought to determine more and more confidential information about him. The intruder whoever it was had known things about him and their search had been very precise. They'd breached several security files that not even his own security team were aware even existed.

Ray Raskal had never had to account for or take responsibility for all the deaths associated with his first company. The directors he'd appointed had been murdered soon after the clients died and had all been taken care off by an professional assassin that he had hired. None of the deaths had been connected in any way, shape or form to him. Most of the deaths had appeared accidental and the two elderly director's had very few family members. Their family members hadn't chosen to pursue any lengthy investigations or even suspected any kind of malicious behavior. He'd walked away from the situation with his reputation unharmed, liberty unrestricted and lifestyle unscathed.

Once he traced the various files the hacker had accessed, he discovered they had also accessed confidential details about Recreation's current clients. What exactly they intended to do with this information at this point in time however, he was totally uncertain. Ray Raskal had been careful he'd moved two thousand miles away before starting again. He'd recreated his identity, even had some facial plastic surgery to adjust his physical appearance and started again with the vast sum of money he'd managed to siphon off from his first company's operations. Prohuman had been formed, developed and was now beginning to flourish.

The intrusion had shocked him, there was now a visible threat to his peaceful, enjoyable existence and the new empire he was building. A threat he could not yet identify which agitated him tremendously. The invisible intruder could access his heavily guarded system and access it in the unimaginable ways that he'd sought to protect himself from. Ray Raskal knew deep within that this intruder was significantly more dangerous to him than any virus was.

Since Ray Raskal's last interaction with Martine he hadn't seen her again, inside the system or outside it. He'd decided to leave the issue of their mutual attraction neglected as he allowed any romantic connection between them to die a slow and painful death. At times he'd watched her waiting around the lounge, aware that she was probably hoping that one day he would return. Inside him however he knew he simply couldn't risk it, he couldn't risk having feelings for Martine, they would weaken him and after the intrusion he now faced that was a risk he just couldn't take.

Ray Raskal sat in his office as he contemplated his next course of action. He knew from the files that had been accessed, this malicious intruder was more than just a jealous fan or a competitor. They had sought out something deeper and he could tell from the areas of the system they had accessed they knew more about him than anyone else at Prohuman Inc. did. They had knowledge, they had information about him and they had managed to connect him with his past. That made them highly dangerous.

There was only one person Ray Raskal knew he could turn to and count on in this situation. Only one person he could turn to and rely on to eliminate this threat. The one person Ray Raskal knew he could trust to handle this dilemma promptly and properly. He picked up his phone and looked at it as he paused for a second. Once he made this call, there was no turning back and that was a reality Ray Raskal was extremely aware off. Once the phone call was made, it was likely that this situation would end in death and that death he was determined, would not be his.

Ray Raskal took a deep breath and prepared to make the call as he scrolled through the numbers on his phone. Finally he found the number he was looking for a made the call as he nodded. This was his only choice and deep down he knew, it was unavoidable now.

A few minutes later a deep, male voice sounded out as the party he'd called, answered his call and greeted him.

"Hello." A familiar male voice remarked a few seconds later.

"Tracker it's me. I need your help." Ray Raskal explained.

"Ray it's been a long time. How are you?" Tracker asked. "Do we still call you Ray or did you change everything on your return from Poland?"

Ray Raskal smiled at Tracker's precision, he'd even remembered where he'd had disappeared to.

"It's still Ray, surname's different though." He replied.

"Great anything you need me to do? I mean I'm assuming this is not a social call." Tracker remarked. "We're not very social people after all are we Ray?"

Ray Raskal smiled briefly at his comment, he knew that it was true. Relief washed over his body refreshing him from the exhaustion of the worry that had been building inside him as it revitalized him like a morning shower. Ray Raskal was relieved, he'd been able to trace him so easily and the situation was now being handled sufficiently. If Tracker had disappeared and he'd been unable to locate him, Ray Raskal would have been stranded and he knew it.

"Your right. I have a job for you." He replied.

"Great when do we start?" Tracker asked.

"As soon as you can. I have an intruder and they have a lot more information about me than I'm comfortable with. I need you to track them down and I need them dealt with." Ray Raskal explained. "They may be working as part of a team and there might be more than one person involved."

"No problem Ray. I'll engage some of my people and get to work straight away." Tracker insisted. "I'll start with two of my men and if the operation needs are greater I'll let you know."

"Thanks." Ray Raskal replied appreciatively, relieved that Tracker had been so enthusiastic about assisting him as he ended the call.

Tracker was the one person he knew he could rely on as long as the money was there and the money was the one thing that Ray Raskal could definitely provide. Tracker would deliver quickly, effectively and professionally. The threat to Ray Raskal and Prohuman would not be a threat for much longer and he was comforted by that thought as he entered into the bedroom at the back of his office and prepared to sleep. It was too risky now he'd decided to leave the building now and return to his home each night, he had no idea when the intruders might strike again and what their objective was, they may even try to kill him, Ray Raskal had speculated. Prohuman HQ was impenetrable physically and heavily guarded. His personal home however he knew had a lot more open ground surrounding it and was definitely less secure. Ray Raskal had decided to stay at Prohuman HQ until the situation was resolved and the threat to his existence eliminated.

Early the next morning as Ray Raskal slept, he received a call from Tracker. He sat up quickly as he answered it full of eagerness and enthusiasm as he forced himself to wake up.

"I've identified your intruders." Tracker remarked. "Two of them are known to your company and the third is a freelance hacker that works on his own. Not a major threat to your operations, but they do have information about your past."

Ray Raskal swallowed nervously as his throat started to feel dry and parse.

"What do they know?" Ray Raskal asked as he feared the answer and response he knew was sure to come.

"They know all about Virtual Humans and they know all about you Ray." Tracker explained.

"We have to meet and soon." Ray Raskal replied. "Do you have their names?"

"I have more than that. I know their names, where they live, where they work, their credit history, every relationship they've ever had and any property they've owned." Tracker replied.

"That was fast." Ray Raskal remarked.

"I'm very thorough Ray and I'm very quick." Tracker said.

Ray Raskal knew it was true, Tracker was the most reliable person he knew when it came to tracking anyone down and finding out anything he needed to know. He was the ultimate professional and though he was pricey, his perfectionism, rapid results and accuracy was unmatched. He was the best in his field and Ray Raskal knew it.

"How would you like me to proceed Ray?" Tracker asked.

"Start with full scale surveillance immediately then we'll decide how to proceed in a day or so. Once we have a full understanding of the precise threat they pose, what they are aiming to achieve and who they are exactly I can decide what I want to do. We have to make sure first they're not working with another third party that is more problematic and powerful. We have to be sure before we take the necessary action, that they're working in isolation." Ray Raskal replied.

"Sure. Let's meet in two days. Any longer than that and you run the risk that they'll start to seek out other third parties to assist them somehow in handling the information they've accumulated. Those third parties may be able to inflict significant damage to you Ray and that's a problem you really don't want to face." Tracker explained.

"Your right." Ray Raskal agreed. "There's a dilapidated warehouse outside of town near

Highway 25. We can meet there on Saturday at noon."

"I'll be there." Tracker confirmed.

Ray Raskal breathed a sigh of relief as he ended the call. He had absolute confidence in Tracker's abilities and was reassured that the threat the intrusion had presented, was now under control. The damage two clients and a freelance hacker could do to him personally was not severe and he knew it. They themselves were not a huge threat but he knew if they managed to leak the information about him they'd uncovered to anyone important, he could potentially lose everything.

Tracker had comforted and appeased him as Ray Raskal began to relax a little. He felt slightly more at ease now as he attended to his tasks and affairs that morning. The situation in his mind was now officially almost under control. Ray Raskal knew Tracker would take any measures required to handle the situation if he felt things were escalating and the threat was becoming more severe. The invisible intruder was no longer invisible and within a short space of time Ray Raskal knew, they'd no longer even be alive.

DEADLY IMPLICATIONS

Martine parked her car in the driveway outside her home. She'd left Jonas with Lamar after their tiring day and was now utterly and totally exhausted. She welcomed the prospect and comfort of her cozy, beautiful, warm bed as she locked the car and gazed up at her lounge window. She glanced around at the street outside, it seemed quiet, empty and dark.

The area Martine lived in was relatively quiet, a middle income type of neighborhood, the fantastically rich and wealthy didn't live there but neither did the drug lords and gangs that often ravaged poorer communities. There was very little crime, most of the neighbors were married with children and it was relatively peaceful. Their gardens were separated by a few hedges and fences and at this time of night most of the neighbors were usually indoors. Tonight was no exception and as Martine stepped away from her car, she realized how very much alone she was in the titillating chill of the dark night.

A noise distracted her and she turned to see what it was, she thought about the possibilities; it could perhaps be a cat, a dog tied up to a kennel nearby or perhaps even a fox. It wasn't unusual for foxes, raccoons and strays to find their way into someone's garden to ravage and scavenge amongst the garbage bins that were situated outside some people's homes. Scavengers of that kind she knew were often hungry and the quietness of the neighborhood often attracted this kind of attention and provided them with an easy meal from unguarded trash cans it housed.

Out of the corner of her eye however as she surveyed the street quickly, she noticed a man a little further down the road dressed in a dark jet, black coat and hat. He seemed to be watching her, his intrusive, peering eyes, burnt into her skin like lasers and prompted her to rush towards her front door more quickly as she trembled with fear.

The door stood silently nearby, oblivious to her alarm and she quickly opened it by pressing her fingerprint into the keypad nervously, she waited a second until the light turned green and the door clicked to indicate it was unlocked. She pushed it open quickly and rushed inside, once inside she closed it quickly behind her and secured another lock in an attempt to make sure, she was very secure. She leant against the back of the door for a second out of breath as her heart pounded in the chest of her ribcage like a fast beating drum.

Martine then made her way to the lounge and picked up her phone to make a call. She hesitated for a moment as she contemplated exactly who she should call. Thoughts flooded through her mind as she realized that calling her family was totally out of the question. She debated the matter further and decided that calling authorities would be difficult as they'd want to know why she hadn't been to see doctors about her health. Finally after a few seconds of further deliberation she determined Jonas was definitely the optimal choice and that he was the best person to call in this situation. She flicked through the numbers on her phone until she found his name and touched the screen to activate the call. He answered her call after a few seconds and Martine breathed a sigh of relief.

"Jonas a man followed me. He's probably still outside. Someone's watching me." She blurted down the phone as soon as he answered it, her words tumbling over each other as her anxiety increased and heightened.

Jonas listened quietly at the other end of the line as she spoke. The realization started to hit him if someone was following Martine, it was possible by now that Ray Raskal knew he'd infiltrated their system and it was highly probably by now that someone may also be watching him. Martine's life may now be at risk and so possibly was Lamar's and his own.

"Don't answer the door to anyone and make sure all the windows are locked. I'm on my way." Jonas insisted.

"Thank you." Martine replied, relieved as he ended the call.

Martine had no desire to be alone right now, she knew someone was out there watching her and perhaps even waiting for her to leave her home again. The possibility of leaving the house to go anywhere alone now was totally out of the question.

Jonas quickly grabbed his car keys and made his way out of the house whilst he walked towards his car, he looked around him anxiously for a moment, to see if he too was being watched or followed. Perhaps they'd been watching him for a while and he hadn't even noticed he thought as he opened the car door and stepped inside. He called Lamar as he shut the car door behind him and started to drive towards Martine's home. Lamar being around now would be beneficial he concluded; he and Martine were both now very physically weak and he knew that if anyone attacked them, there would very little they'd actually be able to do to defend themselves. Lamar on the other hand was strong, physically able and capable unlike them; he hadn't touched the poisonous headsets and his body hadn't been contaminated by the disease that by this point in time had infiltrated every part of their skin. Jonas knew Lamar could give Martine the physical protection that right now he simply couldn't and he sought his presence.

Ray Raskal had decided to have a relaxing evening at home, he'd invited Athena to his home for an intimate evening and was carefully orchestrating his plan towards her. They sat in the lounge as he caressed her arm gently.

"You know Athena, I have a feeling all these troubles will soon be over." He reassured her as he ran a finger down her arm.

Athena smiled enthusiastically as he touched her naked flesh teasingly. She in an inviting manner, removed the cardigan she wore over her dress, to indicate to him that she was ready for him. Athena was ready to surrender her physical body to him and she was making Ray Raskal aware of her passionate desires. He ignored the signal she sent however and continued to prolong their physical consummation. He knew that if he made her wait a little longer and prolonged their sexual intertwining, he would heighten the intensity and sexual intimacy between them, when the actual event occurred. Athena would then as she succumbed to her desires, yield herself to his every desire and requirement. Ray Raskal would then have the leverage he needed over her which would ensure her full compliance with any requests.

Physically Athena wasn't totally his type and he'd decided to compromise in terms of attraction for the potential rewards he felt a relationship between them could bring to fruition. Martine appealed to him much more in terms of attraction, however he knew she had neither the strength or position that Athena had. Ray Raskal knew right now he needed every weapon of defense he had at his disposal and Athena was a much more suitable choice in that respect.

Ray Raskal had absolutely no qualms about utilizing sexuality and attraction to gain power and defend his position, his mind interpreted this as simply something that had to be done to achieve the results he required. Athena was like a baby in his hands as she lapped up the attention he gave her and fed his ego with compliments.

"I know Ray the world just doesn't understand and accept pioneers." Athena had murmured in response seductively and sympathetically as she stroked his leg. "Throughout history geniuses were always chastised." She continued. "We'll get through this."

Ray Raskal smiled at her loyalty and patriotic attitude towards his cause. She'd never asked him about his past and it was unclear if she'd ever even heard of his first company Virtual Humans. The chances she knew about it were remote but possible the only real correlating elements that could connect him, he thought were the services each company offered, which were similar in nature but not totally identical.

Ray Raskal had recently allocated and was lavishing more and more time on Athena, he hoped to develop a deeper, emotional connection to him within her. In the process of doing so, he studied and observed her in order to understand her motivations and how he could induce her loyalty and dedication to him so that it reached optimal capacity. Athena he'd realized was motivated and attracted to power and money, it intrigued her, fascinated her and her weakness enabled him to easily pull her deeper into his web and to ensnare her. Whether she would be willing to sacrifice her ethics to protect him and attain the power she sought in his empire however was another matter he knew may not be fully determined until a later point in time but from what he'd seen up until now, he felt it was likely she would. Athena was not that different from him and deep within they both knew it.

The three men Ray Raskal had assigned to collate information about the intruders that had breached and hacked into the system were giving him regular updates through Tracker. Tracker the man he'd hired to dispose of the directors from Virtual Human Inc. was well known to Ray Raskal and although the other two men weren't, they were Tracker's close contacts and he trusted Tracker's judgement. When Ray Raskal had contacted Tracker with this assignment, he'd engaged the two other men immediately to assist him.

Tracker met Ray Raskal that Sunday as they'd agreed in a run down, empty, depilated warehouse type building outside of the city; it was isolated, remote and abandoned; the perfect location for such a confidential meeting. Ray Raskal had once visited the warehouse when he'd been searching for a location for Prohuman Inc.'s headquarters but hadn't felt it was suitable.

"You have a larger problem than we originally anticipated, they've started seeking out other clients connected to your system. I've installed camera's and listening devices in their homes and tracking devices to their vehicles. Whatever they say or do, I'll know immediately. However that does not solve your problem Ray. They know all about your last company and they are tracing your other clients daily." Tracker explained.

Ray Raskal listened quietly to Tracker as they stood stationary in a corner of the empty warehouse engaged in deep discussion. Tracker as he was called by those who hired him was an ex Special Forces operative. He'd been dishonorably discharged due to being engulfed in a scandal five years before. He'd innocently been caught up in a situation that resulted in ten civilians being shot in the middle of the city in a hostage situation. He'd been used as a scapegoat of blame, though he'd been unaware of all the facts and inadequately briefed going in. He now made a living being hired by corporations and individuals for secret missions which usually involved investigations and quite often murders. Where once he'd been loyal to the government, this had now changed and his loyalties to them had been eradicated. He'd disappeared to Europe, changed his identity and appearance and as far as they knew, he'd never come back.

Tracker provided Ray Raskal with photos and names of the people who had infiltrated the system. He gazed at their photos surprised as Tracker displayed them on a small hand held screen. Martine he recognized instantly and it shocked him. The woman he had been intimate with now looked older, weaker and had rashes all over her skin. Ray Raskal felt a ping of guilt prick his conscience as he looked at her and it strapped itself to his inner soul. He cared little about the other two men but the presence and condition of Martine hit a nerve inside him and he swallowed anxiously. It was the closest he'd ever come in terms of caring about the ramifications of his mistakes and errors. For the first time he started to feel heavy, burdened by the guilt her depilated image presented to him. He'd done this to her, Prohuman had done this to her and he was ultimately responsible.

Tracker looked at him curiously for a moment as he wondered what attachment had prompted Ray Raskal to freeze.

"Everything ok Ray?" Tracker asked.

Ray Raskal sighed and nodded as he shrugged.

"It'll be fine soon." Ray Raskal replied.

He quickly shrugged off the gnawing guilt a few seconds later as if it was an old coat he no longer desired to wear as Tracker showed him the second and third photos. Jonas he remembered vaguely but his presence at the initial induction had been irrelevant to Ray Raskal who rarely remembered client's faces or names unless they were somehow strategically significant. Some clients he took a more active interest in simply because they were premium members. They were given priority and were deemed much more important to Ray Raskal as they provided the most income to the company. He actually made an effort to ensure he remembered all their names and faces without any kind of assistance and at times handled any problems they had personally.

Jonas however was not a premium member, therefore his face had simply faded into a sea of obscurity within Ray Raskal's memory banks, his position there was somewhat arbitrary as it verged on nonexistence but retained a seat very close to the shelf of irrelevance. Lamar's face, he did not recognize at all and Tracker explained to him who Lamar was and the nature of his hacking skills as Ray Raskal glanced at his photo for a moment curiously.

Ray Raskal knew Tracker was expensive but that his services were worth it and the results he'd delivered already were providing him with a blanket of reassurance that he desperately required. The intrusion had made Ray Raskal feel vulnerable and feeling vulnerable was not a feeling that he liked at all. Tracker was thorough, professional and his work impeccable and Ray Raskal knew Martine and Jonas wouldn't present much of a problem for him and neither would Lamar. He smiled as he listened to Tracker explain to him who exactly Lamar was as he wondered why this third party had decided to interject himself into this situation. Aside from a friendship with Jonas he could see no other reason or justification for doing so and Ray Raskal shook his head as he contemplated just how significantly the trio had underestimated who Ray Raskal was, his capabilities and just how far he was willing to go to protect his empire.

"We have to proceed to the next stage." Ray Raskal explained anxiously. "To ensure that Prohuman survives, they have to die."

Ray Raskal knew, the longer he allowed the current situation to exist, the bigger the threat would become.

Tracker nodded in agreement.

Tracker fully understood the threat that Martine, Jonas and Lamar presented. He like Ray Raskal had thought it was unusual that two of his clients had established real friendships with each other, unusual that they had a friend who was a professional hacker and unusual that they'd been able to breach the Prohuman Inc. security system. Yet he concerned himself with the threat they know posed which to him was the more pressing matter and not how they actually met in the first place.

Rapid one of the other men Tracker had hired to assist him, also attended the meeting alongside Tracker. Rapid had assisted Tracker the last time Ray Raskal had, had a problem. Though they'd not been formally introduced throughout the previous operation, this time they actually met face to face. Tracker introduced Rapid to Ray Raskal formally as he started to engage him in the conversation they were having.

"Rapid will help me find a way to dispose of them relatively quietly." He explained. "As far as I know no third parties know about their interactions and connections to each other yet and their murders will be orchestrated in such a manner that they won't be connected to Recreation or you." Tracker reassured him.

Rapid smiled and nodded as he shook Ray Raskal's hand. Rapid's nickname had been given to him by his former associates; prior to joining Tracker, he'd been a hired street killer, one of the best. When Tracker turned Rogue after his dishonorable discharge, he'd hired him and they'd been working together for several years. Rapid's nickname had been given to him for one reason and one reason alone, his ability to orchestrate the rapid murder of any target he was paid to eliminate. He was fast, careful and effective. Tracker had recognized his talent, appreciated his professionalism and skills immensely as soon as they'd crossed path's and he'd hired Rapid almost immediately.

"What about the system itself." Tracker asked as he thought for a moment about how potentially big this assignment might become, if further actions were not taken urgently to curb the threat.

"Are you going to demobilize it until you resolve the problems?"

Ray Raskal looked at him thoughtfully for a moment. He had a lot of clients and the odds were that the contaminated headsets were just part of a bad batch. He'd stringently tested them and most of the batches had passed the tests. He had over five thousand clients and only five people out of those five thousand had been affected so far and Ray Raskal was reluctant to terminate Recreation.

He quickly worked out that they'd all been inducted in the space of a two month period which indicated the health problems were definitely connected to a particular batch of headsets. He couldn't face the prospect of losing Prohuman Inc. or putting Recreation itself out of action for an indefinite period of time. Ray Raskal knew if he shut down the system, he would suffer a loss of clients and business and that was a risk he couldn't afford to take.

Ray Raskal had to make a decision in terms of cost; it made far more sense for him to eliminate the five individuals he'd discovered, that had been affected by the headsets over the course of the next few months, than to shut down his operations indefinitely. He decided he would also make sure all the remaining headsets in that particular batch that hadn't been issued yet, were recalled and stored somewhere outside the city in an obscure, hidden and secure location. Those measures he decided would ensure that no one ever discovered them or could ever connect them to him or Recreation. Destroying them altogether he knew was difficult due to the chemical content they contained.

"No, we'll carry on for now and eliminate the five clients affected." He explained. "I've identified and will resolve the cause of the problem."

Tracker nodded, he motioned towards Rapid and the other man who'd accompanied them who stood quietly nearby as he indicated it was time for them to depart. They started to walk towards the door as Tracker hung back for a moment to walk alongside Ray Raskal. The sauntered together towards the exit and made small talk as they walked.

"Nice nose job by the way." Tracker teased, his tone a little more playful now as he relaxed a little.

Ray Raskal nodded. "Yes I had to have a bit of work done. After the last situation." He explained.

Tracker slapped him playfully on the back and laughed. "It's a definite improvement Ray." He remarked.

Ray Raskal smiled in response, he was very much aware of how he'd intentionally changed his physical appearance to be as pleasing visually to the opposite sex as possible. He'd decided whilst he endured the procedures he'd had to undergo to mask his identity, becoming as physically attractive as possible was an added bonus which would definitely assist him in reestablishing his life and building his new empire. The surgeon had been instructed accordingly and Ray Raskal had been satisfied by the outcome as had the many women who often gave him attention, compliments and smiles as a result of how he now looked.

When Ray Raskal started to establish Prohuman Inc. his improved, enhanced handsome looks had added to the illusion of perfection that that Prohuman Inc. presented. The clean cut looks presented a founder with an exceptionally handsome face which correlated exceedingly well and presented a package and image to clients that represented success, beauty and the possibility of the perfect life, which he knew so many people sought after but in reality could rarely attain. Ray Raskal had incorporated the required plastic surgery he'd had to have into his marketing plan and for the most part he felt his investment seemed to have paid off. Prohuman Inc. had definitely flourished in ways that VirtualHuman hadn't.

The next few days, Ray Raskal spent in solitude as he waited for the call from Tracker to confirm that the situation with Martine, Jonas and Lamar had been resolved and his mission was partially complete. He kept his distance from Athena as he waited, he had no desire to expose his inner thoughts and plans to anyone. Athena he knew was observant and it was possible she may notice his emotional detachment and distance from her due to the distraction, if he spent time any with her and later if it transpired people connected to Prohuman Inc. had died in suspicious circumstances; she may not be as loyal as he hoped. He simply wasn't ready to take that risk. Athena for now he was still unsure about, unsure that their emotional entanglement and physical bond was strong enough yet to endure that type of trial and test.

Tracker put him out of his misery relatively quickly. He called him a few days later to reassure him that things were all under control and that the matter would be taken care off by the weekend.

"We've found a solution regarding the fact that Martine and Jonas know each other. We'll stage their deaths as a robbery and plan it so that they are together when it happens." Tracker explained. "That way we can cover any association they have with Prohuman Inc. and disconnect any kind of link between you and their deaths."

Ray Raskal was delighted by the details of the plan and agreed immediately.

"What about the other one. The hacker." Ray Raskal asked.

"He often visits the male Jonas, we've planned to attack when they are all together at his residence." Tracker continued. "That way it seems impersonal and their murders just coincidental as a result of a random break in."

Ray Raskal was delighted as he ended the call and rubbed his hands together in glee. He'd been absolutely reassured by Tracker that the murders would never be traced back to him and that the situation had now been fully resolved; all he had to do now was wait for the news from Tracker that the executions had actually occurred.

For the next couple of days Ray Raskal attended Prohuman Inc. headquarters as usual once more, relaxed and reassured that any issues would very soon be totally eradicated. Unlike the few days prior to this however he now mingled with the staff more and he even took Athena for lunch on one occasion. He avoided spending any significant periods of time with her however in the evenings due to the fear that he might receive a call from Tracker in her presence.

Martine and Jonas continued to search through the list of clients they'd been given by Lamar. They didn't approach anyone face to face but just located them and observed them as they checked them off one by one according to how they healthy they looked. Most people seemed to be fine and they'd only found one more person that displayed the same kind of symptoms as they did. They'd worked their way through the list and found twenty five of the people named on it so far and only had five more people to track down.

Lamar was meeting them again the next Friday evening, when it had been decided, they'd discuss their findings with him and what they should do next. Martine was unsure about approaching people in person and Jonas was totally against it. He'd been worried ever since he'd discovered that there was a man following Martine and he expressed his concerns as they sat in his car.

They watched as one of the clients they were looking for walked up a nearby street towards where they were situated. Jonas feared doing anything that may cause an escalation in the situation, he had no desire to put their lives at even more risk until he could be sure they had a proper plan that would provide them with protection.

"If they're watching us and we speak to anyone else, we may be exposing them to risk too." He'd explained to Martine when she'd asked what they should do next.

Martine had nodded in agreement. She knew Jonas was right, the night she'd been followed home she'd been terrified. They had no idea what the people following them were capable off and Martine knew deep within she had no desire to actually find out. For now she'd agreed it was better to just collate information and decide what to do with it later.

By the Friday they'd visited all thirty of the people named on the list and found two more people that were affected which now brought the victim count up to five including themselves. Lamar visited on the Friday evening as he'd promised and as they ate pizza in the lounge, Martine showed him the photos she'd taken on her phone of the woman and man they'd found with similar symptoms.

"What do you think we should do now?" Martine asked. "We still haven't found a possible cure yet."

Lamar shook his head.

"I'm not sure yet. There are some very serious implications to this." Lamar remarked. "The people following you. It's very worrying."

Jonas nodded and stood up, deep in thought, he walked over to the nearby fridge and brought out some more beers and a chilled bottle of wine. He returned to the lounge a few minutes later as he handed a chilled, ice cold bottle of beer to Lamar and filled up Martine's glass with more wine.

"Let's wait until Monday and make a decision then. We can do some more research in the meantime for a possible cure over the weekend." He remarked as he sat back down.

Martine and Lamar nodded in agreement.

They continued to talk and research as they searched fervently and earnestly for a cure that deep down they knew may not even exist as the hours of the evening disintegrated into night and darkness began to fall outside. Jonas offered a solution as tiredness set in and the late hours arrived as Martine and Lamar started to display obvious signs of fatigue.

"Martine you can sleep in the guest room and Lamar either you or I can bunk down on the sofa." He suggested. "Save anyone driving home. After all we've all had quite a bit to drink." He paused as if deep in thought before he continued. "Martine I really don't think it's a good idea for you to drive or go home alone this late at night anyway especially after what happened last weekend."

Martine and Lamar nodded in agreement and prepared to spend the night as Jonas disappeared for a few minutes then reappeared with some blankets and a pillow in his arms. Lamar smiled and grinned.

"I'll be good on the sofa." He insisted as he slapped Jonas's back playfully.

Jonas smiled and accepted his humble offer, Lamar was a man and he knew he'd probably slept in worse places just as he had, Martine however he was slightly more worried about. Women could be a little bit more particular about where they slept and quite often didn't really like to spend the night in a man's home, unless they were dating or in a relationship with them. He was anxious to put her at ease.

"I'll show you to the guest bedroom." He remarked as he led her gently by the arm out into the hallway as quickly as he could, before she could possibly object.

Martine was willing and displayed no signs of resistance as she followed him through the hallway and down the few steps nearby which led to the bathroom and two bedrooms situated at the rear of his apartment.

"That's your room." Jonas said as he opened one of the doors and invited her to enter inside.

Martine smiled and entered, she then turned to face him once more.

"Thank you." She remarked as she held the bedroom door and prepared to close it.

Jonas understood her actions immediately. He knew by her actions that she was making it obvious to him that she wasn't interested in him coming inside. He smiled as he thought further, thoughts of romance and passion right now were the last thing on his mind and he knew that Martine had nothing to fear from him in that respect. Right now he had no romantic intentions and there was no pressure on his part. Right now he was far more worried about Martine's safety and his paramount objective was to make sure she felt comfortable sleeping in his home, he had no desire to put her safety in jeopardy in any way, shape or form by imitating or engaging in any kind of sexual or romantic pressures.

Martine closed the door as he turned away and walked the few steps that led to his bedroom as he prepared to sleep. Whilst he was very attracted to her he now felt that, the ship of romance for them had probably already sailed. When he'd stopped calling her as frequently as he should, distracted by Alivia, he knew he'd sacrificed the possibility of a strong romantic bond between them. Martine, he knew was not stupid and she would not accept being second choice to anyone, he'd picked Alivia over her and she'd felt the neglect. Their friendship was now a fully-fledged platonic one and that was unlikely for now to change. They'd crossed the bridge of maybes, perhaps and possibly and now were firmly positioned and planted in the friend zone, like an old aging oak tree that buries its roots deep in the fathoms of the ground, steadfast, unshakable and unmovable.

Jonas prepared to sleep as he undressed and snuggled under his duvet. He embraced it's warmth and sighed in defeat, the battle was over for that day and he'd had to surrender to physical tiredness. Whatever matters they still had to resolve due to the Prohuman Inc. situation, wouldn't be resolved that night, that much he knew. Perhaps in his dreams he could find some sexual stimulation and comfort he thought as he considered for a   moment his past romantic liaisons with Alivia, he closed his eyes as he tried to conjure them up.   Fatigue and tiredness wrapped itself around him like a boa constructor and enveloped his body as he snuggled against the warmth that emanated from the interior of his bed and drifted off into the darkness into the realms of sleep relatively peacefully.

Meanwhile Tracker, Rapid and the third man Hunter, the quietest of the three, stood outside Jonas's apartment block as they quietly watched the building, they prepared for their night as the evening dimmed and darkness approached. They waited for the lights to be disappear in the apartment windows, before they made their way towards the rear of the building. They knew the features of the building and were familiar with the layout by now as they'd scouted it just a few days before. Tracker had managed to get his hands on a blueprint of the layout which had also helped them prepare in advance.

Tracker pulled down the fire escape steps they found at the rear of the apartment block and they started to make their way up towards the first floor where Jonas's apartment was situated. The alleyway at the back of the building was empty and deserted which worked in their favor. They knew the less attention they attracted the better it was for them and they'd crept through the street and alleyway as quietly as possible to avoid attracting any spectators. Tracker had been careful whilst they waited for the right moment to enter inside the building, they'd stayed a slight distance away from the actual apartment block and had kept well out of sight from the entrance. He wanted to avoid the possibility of being sighted by other residents, who may be entering or leaving.

They climbed the steps quietly and approached the kitchen window of Jonas's apartment. Hunter removed a glass torch from his pocket, approached the window and started to burn a hole in it silently. Tracker and Rapid watched as he burnt a hole large enough for them to climb inside. A few moments later they entered inside the building quietly through the gaping hole in the window Hunter had made. Once inside the kitchen, Tracker nodded at Rapid and Hunter who made their way quickly towards the two bedrooms situated at the far rear of the apartment, whilst he proceeded to approach the sofa in the lounge.

Their arms were laden with long, sniper type rifles. The guns were the latest issue in gun technology, they fired a type of bullet that exploded in the person's body upon impact. The pieces and fragments of the bullet, would then travel through the wounded person's internal system and work their way straight to the target's heart and stop it immediately. The high tech weapons ensured their mission would be easier, there would be no noise, no complications and very little mess.

Tracker walked towards the lounge silently and quickly as he observed Lamar nearby fast asleep on the sofa. A few seconds later he walked up to him and fired a shot straight into his chest. Lamar's eyes opened for a split second as he grabbed his chest and then closed again, almost immediately. Death had been instant and Tracker was satisfied.

Rapid who'd by now entered inside the bedroom Martine was sleeping in, paused for a second frozen nervously. He looked at the bed and shook his head as he noticed Martine's face and hair. He took a step forward, pointed the gun at her chest and fired it. Satisfied he'd hit his target, he immediately prepared to leave the bedroom but he paused at the door for a second before leaving and shook his head for a moment before he finally departed. Rapid felt a little dejected by his mission. He'd quickly realized that he'd been unlucky enough to pick the room that was housing the female target, it had been random and either he or Hunter could have borne the task but he'd been unlucky enough to enter the room, Martine was fast asleep in, which meant it had become his mission not Hunters. When he'd seen Martine's hair and face, his conscience had pinged him for a moment. It was one particular aspect of his work he'd never really enjoyed, he thought as he resumed his journey and headed back towards the kitchen. The act of taking the life of a female was particularly hard on him as he knew that usually his assignments involved protecting women not killing them and it burned him inside for a moment that he'd had to orchestrate her murder.

Jonas stirred as Hunter entered inside his bedroom. Hunter paused for a moment as he watched Jonas who lay in the bed in front of him, to ensure he wasn't actually going to wake up. A few seconds later Jonas actually woke up and sat up, he was still drowsy and partially asleep however so he didn't actually notice Hunter's presence. Hunter was taking no chances as he panicked and quickly raised the rifle he held in his arms. He shot Jonas three times in the chest just to make sure he would definitely die. Hunter knew he couldn't risk Jonas realizing he was there, even for a second as he may call out for assistance and alert someone to their presence. A few seconds later as Jonas dropped back down onto the bed still and lifeless, Hunter left the bedroom satisfied.

Tracker, Rapid and Hunter gathered once more in the lounge as they prepared to trash the house and stage the break in. They noticed the laptops situated on a table nearby. Rapid quickly collected them and bundled them into a large bag, he tossed them inside quickly almost as if they were items of trash.

They three then went to and fro throughout the apartment as they emptied Lamar, Jonas and Martine's wallets, bags and purses. They picked up a few other valuables and placed them in the leather bags they carried as they continued to set the stage for the false robbery they had to create. Tracker and Rapid quickly moved towards the bedrooms and started to trash them a bit more chaotically to ensure the burglary look unplanned, frantic and sporadic, whilst Hunter continued to check the rest of the apartment to ensure they'd removed anything that looked remotely valuable.

A few minutes later Tracker nodded towards Rapid and Hunter as he indicated silently that it was time to conclude their assignment. Rapid and Tracker walked quickly back towards the two bedrooms whilst he hung over Lamar and watched him for a moment. Tracker took a burner torch out of his black, leather jacket pocket and pointed it at the bedding and sofa where Lamar's limp, lifeless body lay. He activated it and the flames engulfed the sofa, Lamar and the bedding instantly. Tracker turned and started to walk back towards the kitchen as he waited for Rapid and Hunter to return. They returned a few seconds later and nodded at him as they put their burner torches back into their trouser and jacket pockets.

"Are we finished here?" Tracker asked them seeking verification that the mission had concluded and all the tasks they were assigned had now been orchestrated.

They nodded in agreement.

Tracker quickly made his way over to an ornament situated on a shelf nearby and fished out a camera he'd placed and hidden there on a prior visit. He'd inserted the tiny camera in a slight dip and it had remained concealed and invisible whilst recording every activity that took place inside Jonas's lounge. It was unlikely that anyone who actually searched the house would find the device at a later point in time that much he knew but he'd decided to remove it anyway just in case.

Tracker prided himself on his perfect delivery on any mission he was assigned, he was not a sloppy man and rarely made mistakes. He always cleaned up after his operations and this time was no exception. Tracker satisfied that they had completed the assignment, nodded once more towards Rapid and Hunter and they climbed back out of the hole in the kitchen window then made their way back down to the alleyway outside.

Tracker knew they could have easily let themselves in through the front door and they had advanced technical tools that would allow them to do this very easily but due to the murders, he'd preferred to stage a proper break in and making a hole in the kitchen window had been more consistent with the requirements of this particular operation.

The last time Tracker had broken in to Jonas's apartment to place the camera, he'd actually demobilized the fingerprint lock and entered through the front door, then simply reactivated it once he'd finished. It was less messy, simplistic and much quicker but this time he'd had to actually make more of an effort and stage a more amateur break in.   Tracker was satisfied as they arrived back in the alleyway outside once more that the break in actually looked real and as if it had been orchestrated by professional burglars.

Ten minutes later Tracker called Ray Raskal to confirm the mission was complete.

"The jobs is done."   He explained in a calm tone which lacked any emotion or remorse.

Ray Raskal was relieved as he listened and thanked him.

"I'll put the remainder of your payment into the usual account in a week's time."   He remarked. "As we agreed."

Tracker ended the call as Ray Raskal sat in his bedroom in the pitch dark he smiled with satisfaction, relieved that part of the situation had been taken care off.   He knew he could trust Tracker and his team to locate and silence the other three clients within a short space of time also and that then the matter would be totally resolved. There would be no way to connect Ray Raskal to any of the deaths and he'd planned with Tracker how they would dispose of the other three bodies in a manner that would make their deaths look accidental somehow.

The only death out of the three that Ray Raskal regretted for a second as he sat in the darkness in the still of the night as it's dark fingers poked him with reminders of Martine, was Martine's. The reality now pricked him with remorse and regret and it sat uncomfortably in his mind, unreconcilable with his usual callous nature. She'd been pretty and Ray Raskal knew deep within he'd actually begun to quite like her. Martine though he knew could not live however, she had suffered from the effects of the dangerous headsets and she also knew all about his past. He knew she'd become a threat to his very own existence, a threat that could not coexist alongside him. She was a casualty Ray Raskal would have preferred had not been involved, however the circumstances had been unavoidable and she had become a liability that he'd had to dispose of.

Ray Raskal comforted himself once more by the fact that he'd silenced the voices and the very existence of those who could obstruct him in any capacity. Those who could slaughter Recreation and all that he had achieved. Those who threatened his very own existence and freedom. Prohuman Inc. he was relieved had survived the carnage of his failures and the deadly implications his errors had caused.

PROHUMAN INC.

There had been casualties along the route to survival, but Prohuman Inc. would survive and to Ray Raskal that was his paramount objective. Like a proud father that protected his young, he'd shielded his infant Prohuman Inc. from the threat of being extinguished forever.

Prohuman Inc. would continue to live and breathe and Ray Raskal knew, he would continue to do whatever it took to ensure that Prohuman grew into the corporate, dominating force he'd intended it to be at the time of its inception.

www.ingramcontent.com/pod-product-compliance
Lightning Source LLC
Chambersburg PA
CBHW071307170626
46809CB00001B/360